DECEIVED BISHOP

A.B. COHEN & JP RINDFLEISCH IX

To Boris Sacks Z"L

Tree of Life

Divine One
Keter
Holy
Timekeeper
Binah
Time
Traveler
Chochmah
Space
Elemental
Gevurah
Nature
Lover
Chesed
Heal
Seer
Tiferet
Vision
Invulnerable
Netzach
Sheild
Pacifist
Hod
Hold
Bonded
Yesod
Link
Warrior
Malchut
Push

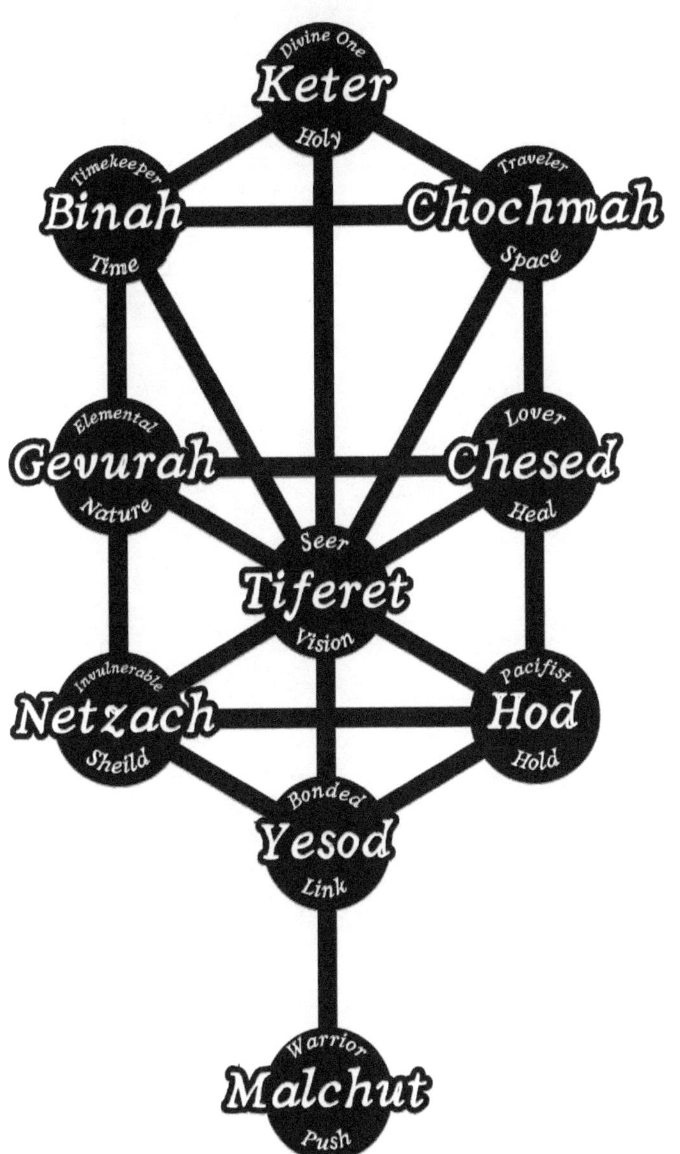

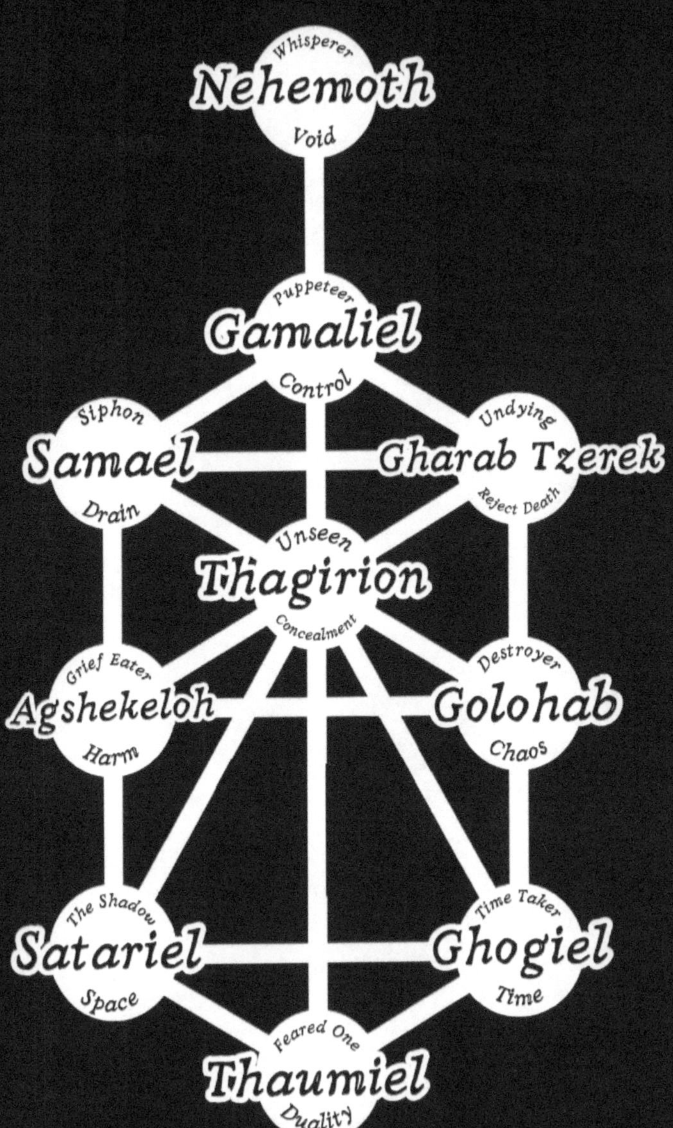

Tree of Death

The Infinity Board

 King

 White Queen

 Black Queen

 White Rook / Sage

 Black Rook

 White Bishop

 White Knight

 Black Bishop

 Black Knight

 White Pawn

 Black Pawn

 Square

CHAPTER I
STATUS QUO

Leah watched the night sky give way to a purple dawn as old and tattered farmhouses passed by her window. The truck slowed and turned, leaving the smooth asphalt for rough gravel roads.

Leaning back, Leah pulled her long brown hair up into a bun. She looked around the truck as she adjusted her thick leather jacket, the hidden knives poking at her side. Her uncle Eric sat at the wheel, and White Bishop Grace sat in the passenger seat, while Joanna, Sarah, and Leah squeezed in the back. A twinge of hope sparked inside her chest, and she frowned. The feeling was not quite her own. She'd gotten better at discerning that.

She looked into the rearview mirror and caught her uncle's eyes. His amber eyes, the same color as hers, were dark and lined with bags. They'd been at this for months, tracking down demons and looking for their leader known as Legion. Every lead had been a dead end, and now Leah felt like they were chasing smoke. Yet, Eric still had hope.

A nudge in her ribs pulled her from her thoughts, and she looked at her friend, Sarah. The white leather jackets they wore made a stark contrast to Sarah's dark skin. Ever since they'd gotten them, Sarah had sat up straighter, and she'd tied her mass of tightly curled hair into a bun like Leah's. She leaned over and whispered, "You ready for this?"

"Ready as I'll ever be. Do you think we're close?" Leah asked, looking out the front window.

Sarah shrugged and nodded to Eric's phone resting on the center console. "His signal went out twenty minutes ago. Should be soon though, as long as we don't get lost."

"We're not lost," Eric grumbled from the driver's seat, slowing down as the road met an intersection and eying the sign.

"I have a good feeling about this one. We've got to make it one of these times." Sarah said.

Leah looked out the window. "Yet we've been at this for months with nothing to show for it."

Grace turned from the passenger seat and reached behind her seat, smacking Joanna on the leg. "You're both starting to sound like this one. Hey! Wake up, sunshine, we're almost there."

Joanna shifted in her seat, pushing back her black hair, then crossing her arms as she glared at Grace. "Ugh, who kills people at this hour?"

Eric looked out the window toward the horizon. "Dawn ritual. The first rays of light hold power."

"Well, so does midnight, or sundown. Why does it have to be a cult that prefers mornings?"

Eric ignored her and turned down a dirt path leading into the forest. Trees shrouded the truck as he came to a stop and killed the engine. "Should be just down this road. We'll take the rest on foot."

Grace pulled a gun from her side holster and checked it over, loading a bullet into the chamber. "Alright then, we're here. Check your stuff and get out."

Leah unbuttoned her holster and wrapped her hand around her gun. She'd checked it before they left, but habit made her pull back the slide and check the chamber, confirming the bullet was still there.

Sarah and Joanna did the same while Grace tapped on her earpiece. "Mic check."

Joanna jumped, yanking out the earpiece, and adjusting the volume. "Heard you load and clear."

Eric nodded to Grace and placed his hand on his door. "Three, two, one." On one, Joanna and Leah popped open their doors and slipped out.

The darkness in the forest brightened, and Leah's eyes grew warm as she called on *Tiferet*, the well of the Seer. The dull grays of the early morning shone back at her with an intensity that let her see individual leaves from a tree nearly fifty yards away.

Movement caught her attention off in the trees, and she lifted her gun. Her eyes homed in on the spot, and a blob of light came into focus. Two squirrels chased each other across the tops of the branches, their tails flicking back and forth.

Without *Tiferet*, she knew even that would have been invisible to her, and she would instead wave her gun at the sound of rustling leaves. Yet, with it, she could home in, seeing every detail in a glowing black-and-white image.

She lowered her gun and spoke into her earpiece. "Clear."

"Clear," Joanna said shortly after.

Eric, Grace, and Sarah got out of the truck and moved into position with Grace and Eric in front, Leah and Joanna protecting the flanks, and Sarah protecting the rear.

The sun shone through the tops of the trees and brought the woods to life. Leah did all she could not to focus on the beauty, but with *Tiferet*, it was hard not to. She caught sight of a cardinal, a stark red among green leaves, preening before letting out a long trill. She could stare at it all day, watching it as it went about without knowing the horrors that plagued nearby.

"K2 in position," a voice sounded through the earpiece.

Leah knew that voice coming through her earpiece, a black woman with dreadlocks and a stern look on her face that could strike you to silence in an instant. Nykima. A White Knight, and ex to her uncle, led the other team positioned at the other end of this patch of woods.

Eric leaned close to Leah and whispered, "Ready?"

Leah gripped her gun and nodded. She wanted this one to be different from the jobs before. She needed it to be different.

Grace raised her hand, and the group collectively held their breath. She brought her arm down and signaled them forward with a quiet, "Move out."

CHAPTER 2

GRAVE

Leah moved in line with Eric, her eyes searching the perimeter of the woods. The deeper they traveled into the woods, the heavier the air became until the familiar stench burned at Leah's nostrils.

She sensed a bonfire up ahead, and the scent of cooked meat and burnt hair was palpable. This was déjà vu, Leah thought to herself. Another mission, another failed attempt. Leah found the other team up ahead in a small clearing, their guns drawn as little pinpricks of yellow eyes glowed.

A voice sounded in her ear. "No signs of life."

Bile rose in Leah's mouth, and an icy chill poured over her as Sid's voice spoke over the earpiece. The man she'd thought was behind the disappearances at the academy but who turned out to be investigating it just like she was.

She spotted him in the center of the group. A tall Black man with short-cropped hair. Beside him stood Isaac, Gabe, and Ricardo.

Isaac flashed Leah a half-hearted smile. His otherwise green eyes looked strange with a yellowed glow, which only made his pale skin and long blond hair seem out of place.

Months on the road had taken a toll on him as well, his already wiry frame thinning with each month that passed. He was the third of Leah and Sarah's closely knit group of friends, and the smallest of all the Pawns in the Queen's Gambit.

Beside him was the last person from the original Black Hills Outpost. Gabe towered over Isaac, his broad shoulders now filling out with muscle. He smiled at his girlfriend Joanna but quickly looked away when Sid cleared his through and muttered, "Stay focused."

Aside from Queen Helen and Constance, the White Bishop who was third in command of the Queen's Gambit and remained back at the academy, the whole team was assembled. Leah accounted for the last three Pawns who made up the team: Brandon, the bully who'd picked on Isaac until his two goons left; Miranda, a "by the book" soldier who could nearly beat anyone in a sparring battle; and Ricardo, the Venezuelan wild card Leah knew practically nothing about.

Nykima locked eyes with Grace across the clearing and nodded. The teams pressed forward, breaking through the trees.

Not again, Leah thought, looking left and right. Inside the clearing was a small cabin and a makeshift fire pit. No signs of life glowed from the cabin as Grace stepped inside, nor from the corpse tied up to a tree near the fire pit.

Leah approached, covering her nose from the putrid smell of burnt flesh. The body was that of a naked woman, likely in her thirties, her charred body pulled tight against the restraints that held her. A deep cut started at the bottom of her chest and drew a clean line all the way down, exposing what remained left inside. Blood still dripped from the wound, and Leah guessed that the woman would still be warm to the touch.

"Confirmed, the site's empty. Mission failed," Grace said, stepping out of the cabin and approaching Eric.

Leah let out a sigh and holstered her gun. She let *Tiferet* drop, colors dulling and blurring as the morning sun shone through the trees.

"Fuck this shit," Brandon said as he kicked a small rock to Leah's left.

Nykima's voice boomed over the earpiece. "Watch it, Roe. Your mic is still on."

Brandon glared in her direction and took out his earbud, stuffing it into his pocket before crossing his arms and leaning against a tree, kicking at the dirt.

Leah walked to the fire, the stench of decay and charred meat intensifying with every step. The flames burned in the middle of several concentric circles dug into the ground, encompassing the tree holding the body as well. At the cardinal directions, small mason jars of dead animals rested half buried in the earth. At the center of this ritual, where the fire still burned, sat a blob which Leah knew was the missing organs from the body. Her vision was blurred, a consequence of using *Tiferet,* and she was thankful she couldn't see the carnage with full clarity.

She paused for a moment, then kicked dirt into the lines dug into the ground. Nothing happened. No rise in winds, no grounds shaking . . . nothing. She wondered if anything actually happened when the demons performed these rituals, since residual energy should have built up. Something would have to happen.

Grace and Eric joined Sid and Nykima at the opposite side of the corpse, whispering indiscernibly.

Eric took a step back, one hand on his waist while he pinched the bridge of his nose and looked up at the sky.

Sarah started toward the trees, her knuckles white as she clenched her fists. Leah caught sight of Gabe approaching Joanna who rolled her eyes at him and joined Sarah at the tree line instead.

Gabe crossed his arms and approached Leah, his voice shaking. "What do you think this all means? These demons just keep getting away with it, vanishing before we even show up."

Joanna tutted her tongue and plopped down on the grass behind them. "That's because it isn't just demons. Chimeras, just like the ones who took me, they're working with the demons. They'd know we're coming from miles away."

Miranda leaned against a tree and flipped a knife over in her hands. "We don't have any evidence that chimeras are involved, nor has the Infinity Board suggested it as a possibility."

Joanna shook her head. "And the Board thought chimeras were extinct until a few months ago. So, don't you think they wouldn't know the evidence if it slapped them in the face? Or did you forget the whole trio of rule breakers over here doing the Infinity Board's job for them and figuring out who was kidnapping us?"

Ricardo shrugged. "Chimeras are mindless beasts. I bet it's easy for the demons to train them as their watchdogs. Or shifters. Sid has been trying to track the pack that attacked my family, but there are so many of them now, it's damn near impossible. Either way . . ." He nodded at the corpse. ". . . something did that to her. Something not human."

"Like I already said," Miranda started, "there's no evidence that suggests shifters, either. They don't even come this far north. Last I heard, there was one in Texas."

Brandon elbowed past Miranda and shoved Ricardo's shoulders. He was at least a foot taller, but Ricardo crossed his massive arms. "Chimeras are not mindless beasts. My brother is not a mindless beast. If you say that again, I will make you regret it."

The sound of a gunshot resonated from Leah's memory, and the furred face of Theodore flashed in her mind as the life left his eyes. Leah spun on her foot, facing the corpse, and looked at Brandon as he droned on about chimeras.

He still believed his brother was alive. Still held on to the idea that he'd find him. Nykima was supposed to tell him the truth months ago. Leah wondered how Nykima could avoid how torturous this was for Brandon. How unfair it was for Leah to carry that guilt around. She couldn't look at him without seeing Theodore's face, his pupils widening as he fell to the ground.

Leah blinked, her vision clearing, and found Isaac crouched next to the body, his arms crossed and hands shaking. She approached him and reached out a hand, resting it on his shoulder.

"Hey, Isaac, are you—"

Isaac cut her off. "Why do we all think this is just normal? Bickering about assignments while there is a dead body strung up right next to us. It's not right. It's . . ."

Nykima and Sid's voices grew louder behind her as their argument for whose tactics failed the mission rose.

Leah traced her eyes from the arguing adults to the arguing Pawns. Everyone seemed too caught up in pointing fingers. No one seemed to care . . . except Isaac.

Leah squeezed Isaac's shoulder and walked past him while taking out her knife and cutting the ropes that tied the corpse to the tree.

Isaac looked up. "What are—"

The sound of a body slamming down onto the ground cut off his questions.

Silence pierced through Leah's concentration, and the bickering stopped altogether. She didn't look. Instead, she pulled a handkerchief from her pocket and tied it around her neck, covering her nose and mouth from the scent of the body as best she could. Then she used her knife to score the ground. Once it was loose enough, she dug, intermixing *Malchut* with her bare hands to tear out large heaps of dirt.

She should have done this the countless times before instead of leaving their poor bodies out to rot. It wasn't right. She didn't care how long it would take; this anonymous person would at least get a proper burial.

Nykima's voice shouted from behind her. "Pawn Ackerman, what are you doing?"

"I'm burying this body."

"The Infinity Board needs us to collect all pertinent evidence for their review. You're wasting your time."

"They have plenty of bodies like this one already. It won't make a difference." Leah continued digging her hands into the dirt, feeling the cold, wet earth accumulated under her nails.

Isaac knelt beside her and started digging. In seconds, Sarah and Gabriel took a knee as well and joined in.

Nykima took a step forward and shouted, "What are you—"

Leah looked over her shoulder and spotted Eric's hand wrapped around Nykima's arm, holding her back.

"Let them. Let *us*. I think we *all* need to remember why we're doing this."

Eric walked past Nykima, knelt beside Leah, and started digging. Before long, the rest of the squad joined in and made a grave suitable to give the body a proper rest.

CHAPTER 3
QUESTIONS

The hot water flowed over Leah, melting into her muscles and washing off the caked blood and grime that covered her. Once they'd arrived back at the academy, she'd waited until the other girls had showered, wanting the space to herself. Now the steamy bathroom carried the scent of hot copper, the stench of blood. She grabbed the bar of hotel soap she had smuggled on their last adventure out of the academy and lathered it in her hands. Citrus cut through, masking the odors left-over from the failed assignment. It was way better than the soap they had in the shower dispensers, and the bubbles dragged the dirt free from her body.

Leah closed her eyes and allowed her mind to wander. Even though she tried thinking of anything else, the image of the woman's corpse was still burned in her mind, tied to a tree, body torn to shreds. Leah's eyes snapped open, her heart racing. Then she took several deep breaths and squeezed her eyes shut again. She tried avoiding the image of the woman, but another replaced it. A man not much older than her. Every time she blinked, another body flashed in front of her eyes. She slid down the shower stall and wrapped her arms around her knees.

Leah had lost count, each corpse always the same, dead before they'd arrived at the scene. And always with the same look of horror and pain frozen on their faces. How much longer could she take it?

She held on tight to her knees, and the serpent inside her chest rose, pressing against her skin.

How many lives had to be torn apart before they could catch these murderers? If she got her hands on even one of them, she'd get the answers they needed. Maybe then they could save someone, for once. Maybe then she could feel like they were actually getting somewhere, instead of cleaning up the mess the killers left behind, taking the bodies elsewhere, covering up the murders so the police didn't get in their way.

It wasn't fair. It wasn't right. She dug her nails into her legs, the pressure inside her building up. She had to contain herself, had to hold it in, but it was too late.

A tiny fraction of pressure released before she got control, bursting out of her in a single, minute pulse.

Water flew away from her in all directions, slamming into the tiled walls with a force that cracked some of them. The soap dispenser jutted free from the wall and clattered to the ground, and the metal shower head bent upward, away from Leah.

"Fuck!" she cried, pounding her fists onto the tiled floor.

Her left arm throbbed for a quick second, and a familiar voice spoke in her head, *Losing control again?*

Leah breathed in through her nose, focusing on the pressure that was built up inside her. She let out a breath and forced it back into her chest, forcing the serpent back into its slumber.

"I'm fine," Leah replied after a few moments.

Asmodeus, the demon that had killed her parents. The demon that now lived within her, making her his last-ditch effort before being consumed by the very demon the Queen's Gambit was after.

He laughed inside her mind. *I can see that.*

"Just shut up, okay? You don't talk for weeks, and now what? You want to criticize me."

Not quite. I—

Leah squeezed her eyes shut and pressed her hands against the side of her head. The images of the dead swirled around, one face after another, but she pushed past it. She focused on Asmodeus, on that feeling in her arm that traveled up to the back of her neck and shouted, "Shut up! Shut up! Shut up!"

Silence echoed back, and Leah sat naked on the shower floor, water spraying on her from the broken shower head.

Leah put her damp hair up in a bun and entered the library, walking past rows of shelves until she found the little nook that had become the hangout for Pawns. The library was meant for a school, with bookshelves and tables meant for well over a hundred Pawns and others who came in. Now that the academy was closed, the library rarely had over ten people in it at a time, and it had become the prime spot to hide from the Knights and Bishops.

She spotted Gabe first, balancing his chair on two legs while he leaned against the wall. His arms weren't as muscular as Ricardo's, but as he held them behind his head, she couldn't help but stare, heat building on her face as he started talking.

"I don't really care," Gabe said. "After all this time, we needed to feel something again. Who cares what Nykima thinks?"

Leah rounded the corner and found Sarah lying down on a big leather sofa while Isaac leaned against the back of it, looking out the window.

Sarah juggled a wad of paper, tossing it up and down. "Honestly, what are they gonna do? They've been screwing things up from the beginning. We have no leads. The only thing we've been good at is showing up after the party and seeing the mess they left behind." Sarah and looked right at Leah, the balled-up paper bouncing off her face. "You plan on creeping in the corner or want to join us?"

Gabe nearly fell out of his chair as he scrambled to land it back on all fours, dropping his arms and clearing his throat. His face turned red as he looked at her and said, "Hey . . . we were just talking about—"

"I heard. Doesn't matter, I already did it. I can't take us showing up when they're all gone anymore." Leah crossed the room and lifted Sarah's legs to plop down on the couch before letting her friend's legs rest back down across her lap.

Sarah nodded. "Nykima claims she was just following orders, but come on, what more could they find that we didn't already know?"

Leah looked over at Gabe. "Where's everyone else? Where's Joanna?"

Gabe shook his head and let out a sigh. "Miranda dragged Ricardo out for some sparring. Poor guy looked beat already, but whatever. Brandon is sulking in his room or whatever, and Joanna keeps ignoring me. Last I saw, she was with one of the guards."

Sarah punched his knee. "She's flirting with him. Trying to get you jealous. Come on, *boyfriend*, can't you see?"

He rubbed his eyes with the palms of his hands. "I don't understand girls."

Sarah laughed. "Hell, I'm one and I don't understand them either. But Joanna's in a league of her own."

Leah stared at Isaac as he continued to look out the window at the cloudy sky. "And what about you, Isaac? How are you holding up?"

He shook his head, pulling himself out of whatever daydream he was in. "Same as all of you, I guess."

He didn't say any more, nor did he have to. Leah suspected he was worse off than she was, and his actions only solidified that thought in her mind. With each corpse they found, he became more and more quiet and reserved. Leah wondered how many more he could handle before it overwhelmed him and he snapped.

Sarah grabbed hold of the wad of paper and tossed it up again. "Yeah, I'm pretty sure we're all ready for this to be over."

It hurt hearing them as defeated as she was. It made her sick and frustrated that she couldn't do anything to help them. She rubbed her temples with her fingers, the pressure in her chest quivering before she began taking slow breaths. "We had two jobs: research the rituals and hunt down the chimeras to get Paige back. Yet, all we've been doing is tracking down ritual after ritual. Did they just forget about the chimeras? Maybe we'd be better off finding a lead there."

Asmodeus echoed in her mind, taunting her. *Now there's an idea.*

Leah shook her head and frowned.

Gabe looked at her and raised his eyebrow. "Yeah. For all we know, they're related. Maybe they think that too, so they aren't even trying to investigate it."

Sarah sat up on the sofa and tossed the paper wad at

Gabe's head. "So, what you're saying is that Joanna might be right? Probably would have been a good thing to have said that to her earlier."

Gabe glared at Sarah and picked up her wad of paper, squeezing it in his fist and tossing it over his shoulder and out of sight. "But I'm still hung up on why chimeras would tear people apart like that. They were human once. I can't imagine they're the ones tearing into the bodies. Unless someone forced them to do it."

Isaac spoke slowly, still focused outside. "Chimeras made a deal before with Dean Wright. Who's to say they wouldn't make another one with Legion?"

Leah felt her heart leap in her chest. Of course. Why didn't she see it before? Why wouldn't they? "Have you told anyone else this?"

Isaac shrugged. "No. Joanna just had me thinking. I mean, they kidnapped her, and she almost became one herself. Since she was gone the longest, I figured she'd know more than us about what they are capable of."

Sarah shook her head, "But there can't be that many. They were extinct. Do you think Paige is in on it? Do you really think she'd be capable of . . . ?"

Images of Paige flipped through Leah's mind. Paige Jones, the girl who'd bullied her until Ian, a corrupted Black Knight, kidnapped her by dragging her away. Then Dr. Toppen, a chimera with octopus tentacles hidden underneath her coat, had turned Paige into some golden-haired beast. Paige was a bully, but underneath her bitchy facade, she cared. Leah shook her head. "No. If it is chimeras, I don't think Paige could be in on it. At least, not deliberately."

Gabe leaned back in his chair again. "I bet they don't all work together. You guys said the doctor was making more chimeras, right? Who's saying she's doing it alone? There could be dozens out there at this point."

Isaac turned from the window and stood up. "We've found no evidence of that, nor has the Infinity Board. That suggests chimeras aren't at the rituals, but that doesn't rule them out. They could easily be nearby, watching and waiting for us to show up. We have searched no farther than a couple hundred feet from the scene. I'll bet the Infinity Board does the same. If we just broadened our search, we could—"

"S'up, Mystery Team featuring Gabe?" Joanna's voice called from the bookshelves. She jumped out and pulled Gabe's chair, nearly knocking him over before pushing him back up and leaning on his shoulder.

"Where were you?" Gabe asked. "I thought you were going to study with us."

Joanna backed up and frowned. "I don't know, *Dad*. I've been around." Her face smoothed over as she looked at Leah. "Grace is looking for all of us. Wants to do some training, I guess. Field two in five."

Leah stretched her arms and pushed off Sarah's legs before standing and cracking her knuckles. "Great, looks like two showers today. Just what I wanted."

Her friends followed suit, joining her as she reached the entrance of the library. Leah turned, a smirk on her face. "Hey Sarah, you think you can save some of the hot water for the rest of—" The words fell as her eyes landed on a pale face peeking out from one stack.

"Absolutely not. The hot water is all mine." She frowned and turned to look at the stacks.

The pale boy vanished from Leah's sight, and Sarah cocked her head.

"Everything okay?" Sarah asked as the others turned as well.

"Yeah, sorry. Go on without me. I think I forgot something." Leah started back toward the stacks.

"Suit yourself."

Leah waited until she heard the door to the library close behind her, then she called out, "Hello, are you there?"

Silence.

She started down the shelves of books, noting the section she had seen the pale boy in. When the academy was still up and running, this section would have been off limits to students. Now it was just another row of dusty books. She called again. "Look, I'm here if you want to—"

A handful of books tumbled off the shelves to her left, piling in front of her. She stepped forward. "I just want to—"

Another shelf shook.

"Fine," she said, holding up her hands. She knelt, collecting the books that had fallen. Their bindings were frayed and barely held them together. All but one, a faded red leather book with gold filigree scrawled over the top. She flipped open the book, eyeing the title. *De Corruptionis Virginum*. She scoffed. "The Virgin's Corruption?"

Her arm tingled, and Asmodeus spoke in her ear. *The corruption of maidens. But yes, you weren't too far off.*

Leah flipped through the pages, which were stained and marked with images of cadavers and depictions of the tree.

You might want to put this one back. I can tell by the softness of the leather that this book is not made from one of your domesticated creatures.

She ran her fingers along the cover. "Then what's it made of?"

Only the flesh of a human could feel so supple, he whispered.

Her stomach turned over, and she slammed the book

shut, placing it back on the shelf. Leah stared down the aisle, half expecting to see the once-pale boy now transformed into his monstrous self. Instead, she saw nothing.

"Fine, if you don't want my help, then you won't get it," she said, turning and leaving the library.

CHAPTER 4

PROMISES

Leah floated in a vast, dark ocean of nothingness. The same place she had been for months. A place void of dreams, where she waited, endlessly, until she woke the next day.

An explosion rumbled through her body, and she opened her eyes, peering out into the inky black sea. She held onto her chest, a memory surfacing of her father hovering over her as they stood together in a doorway. They'd been vacationing in San Francisco when an earthquake hit. She could feel his arms around her, smell the minty sandalwood and hit of oak in his cologne.

The rumbling stopped, and the memory faded back into darkness. Her heart beat loudly in her ears, a thrumming that grew louder with each passing second.

She couldn't lie there anymore, couldn't enjoy the vast nothingness with the pounding of her heart so loud in her ears. She stirred, and with it, more memories flooded into her. Blood, entrails, and corpses filled her mind. The once-calming ocean of black became a pool of blood that Leah would soon enough drown in.

She sat up, and the world shifted. A marble bench

surfaced from the depths of the ocean, and she felt solid ground inches below the water's surface. She sat on the bench in front of a small white stone table that had also emerged. The black ocean lapped at her ankles, and the vast darkness stretched around her. But here it was different.

Her arm tingled for a moment, and Asmodeus's voice sounded behind her. "I suppose since you wouldn't let me come to you, I'd finally wake you here."

A handsome pale-skinned man with dark hair slicked back and blackened eyes stepped out from the shadows across the table from Leah. He straightened his black tie, which blended in with the matching shirt and suit he wore. He took a seat at the opposite side of the table and wrapped his abnormally long fingers around a mug of tea, which materialized before her eyes, steam carrying spices like cinnamon and clove.

"Is this what you really look like?" Leah asked.

Asmodeus took a sip of the tea and locked eyes with Leah. "I don't really know anymore. I once was a being of stone from a realm far away, but this is the form that suits me now."

She eyed his hands while he rubbed them together, the long fingers sending a shiver down her spine. "What did you mean by 'finally waking me?' I'm asleep, aren't I?"

Asmodeus nodded. "You have a special gift. One that could get us in trouble if you were to use it now. Especially when *he* is looking for you. I'm not ready to face Legion, nor are you. I've been keeping you in the sea, keeping you from visiting anyone who might cause you harm."

"And that's what's keeping you quiet? You've been spending all your time holding me back from dreaming, making sure I don't have nightmares? I called you. More than once. I needed help, and you weren't there."

Asmodeus tutted his tongue and shook his head. "You

don't get it, not yet. We can defeat Legion. Once we know what he's doing, I'm sure of it. Just not yet."

"That doesn't answer my question," Leah spit through gritted teeth.

"Your dreaming makes us both vulnerable. Anything that happens to you, happens to me." Asmodeus nodded to Leah's arm, where she could now see the black hand wrapped around it, marking her to him.

"So, that's it then? You only need to keep yourself alive? Those dreams could have pointed us to Legion weeks ago. We could have stopped them. We could have saved . . ." Her voice cracked, and she clenched her fists.

The demon leaned back in his chair, crossing his arms. "Until we are both ready, and you are prepared to be cautious, you will remain trapped here, in this sea of nothingness. Until then, don't try anything, or you may wind up hurt, or worse."

Leah's fist tightened, her knuckles turning white. He'd been holding her back, hiding from her something that could have stopped Legion in his tracks. Pressure uncoiled from her chest and traveled down to her hands. She slammed her fists onto the table, cracking it in half before the whole thing disappeared. "How about you help me track down Legion? He almost ate you. Why are you holding me back from finding him? Do you want more people to die at his hand?"

Asmodeus crossed one leg over the other and rested his hands on his knee. "He knows you are a dreamer. Do you not remember all the times he's turned his eye on you when you're watching him? He'd have ways of trapping you now, ways to keep you from knowing where he is. Last time he caught you, he almost killed you. Would have, if it weren't for me. But that little trick won't work twice. My power has been slowly coming back, but I am in no place to face him. Not yet."

The images of the corpses flashed before her eyes, one after the other. This demon, that had once chased her across the country to find and kill her, was now so pitiful. So weak.

"You are a parasite. A flea. Stop holding me back. I'll be careful. You owe me that much, at least, for what you've done."

Asmodeus let out a sigh and stood, pacing in the shallow waters. "Seems you weren't ready. Not yet. What's done is done. I feel your anger. Your rage. Yet, we are one now. We must face this together." He placed his hands in his pockets, turned, and walked into the shadows.

The waters rose, sweeping Leah back into darkness.

Leah opened her eyes to the white ceiling of her bedroom. Cold sweat seeped through her clothes and made her teeth chatter as she stood and peeled off the layers.

His voice still resonated in the air. *We are one now, we must face this together . . .*

She couldn't accept it. She stood in a damp tank top and shorts while she balled up fresh pajamas in a towel. Turning, she left for the common room, pausing and opening a window to take in the night air before showering.

The cool air brought in the scent of pine, and she let it carry her off in memories of a time before the outpost. A time back when she lived in Chicago.

"I just wish it could be the way it was," Leah muttered to herself. "Why won't you just leave me alone?"

A voice called out from the dark. "Hey, couldn't sleep?"

Leah reared her head, spotting Sarah's silhouette entering from the entrance to the common room.

"Yeah. Needed some fresh air. You?"

Sarah crossed the room and held up a half-eaten scone. "Midnight snack. I figure what's a few more carbs after training?"

Leah smirked and looked back out the window.

"What? No 'hey, didn't you bring me one?'" Sarah reached around to her back pocket and pulled out a second scone, wrapped in napkins. "I even came prepared. I mean, that or this was gonna be seconds."

Leah rubbed at her arm, a lump forming in her throat before she could even get the words out. She turned, looking down at Sarah's feet while tears welled up in her eyes. "I just . . . I don't know where to . . . where to even start."

Sarah set the scones down and wrapped her arms around Leah. "Hey, I can't have you losing it too. Dealing with Isaac is hard enough. Let's just sit here. I'll listen to whatever you have to say. Or we can just hang instead."

Warm arms comforted Leah, and as they broke free from the hug, she nodded. "I've been keeping a secret. Not even Eric knows."

Sarah leaned in and handed Leah the uneaten scone. "It's okay, seriously. You can tell me anything."

Leah picked at the scone and said, "It's Asmodeus. He isn't gone. He's still here."

Chunks of scone fell from Sarah's hands. Her eyes widened, and she looked around the room. "Still here? Where?"

Electricity bristled in the air, and goosebumps traveled up Leah's arms. She couldn't see it, but she knew Sarah had called upon *Malchut*, ready to fight. Leah stuck out her hand. "No. No. Not *here*." She pointed to her arm, and then her head, "Here, in my head. In my dreams."

The sense of electricity died down as Sarah raised an eyebrow. "Like possessing you?"

Leah took in a quick breath. "He marked me the night my parents died. He was hunting me in my dreams. That's how he found us at the outpost."

Sarah shook her head. "But Alma. She bound him to her; she dragged him to his death."

Leah nodded, the memory of Alma, her first teacher, surfacing in her mind. The one who had sacrificed everything to save her students. "She did. At least, she almost did. Legion called him back. I was there, in a dream. Asmodeus, he . . . reached out, touched me . . . before Legion ate him. I think whatever he did, it left a part of him inside me."

"How do you know he's there? Do you see him? Does he talk to you?"

"He was only a voice before tonight. I saw him in a dream." Leah scoffed. "He actually looked . . . human. And maybe even a little handsome? It was freaky. I've only heard his voice until now. And what he's said was helpful."

Sarah took a step back. "Helpful? He killed your parents. Don't you want revenge? We should tell someone. We need to get this little worm out of you before—"

"No," Leah said, "I know what he is. What he did. But he's trapped inside me, not the other way around, and I like knowing that he can't hurt anyone else. Not anymore. He's the one that helped me get that monster off Joanna. He also saved me from Legion when I dreamt of Ian's execution. And at the boathouse, he called Eric for help by using the *Yesod* bond. He isn't completely useless."

"But you're seeing him now? So, he's getting stronger, isn't he?"

Leah looked out the window and watched the trees swaying in the moonlight. "I think so. He's been blocking my dreams. Said it was to keep us safe from Legion, but . . . I don't know. The dreams could be helpful."

Sarah paced back and forth for a long time before pausing and turning to Leah. "I think I would have done the same thing. But do you think we should tell someone now, maybe Constance? She might know something about this. If it is what you say, that doesn't sound like a possession."

Leah shook her head. "I can't even get myself to tell Eric, let alone anyone else. Asmodeus can shield himself. I'm not even sure they could remove him if they tried."

"But they could try . . ."

A throb pulsed in Leah's arm. "No, not yet. If they can't remove it, they'd have to report to the Infinity Board. Then I can only assume I'd be strapped to a dissecting table while they try to figure out how we bonded." Leah reached for Sarah's hands, tears welling up in her eyes from somewhere dark and foreign. "Please. Promise me you won't say anything. Please?"

Sarah looked Leah up and down before speaking slowly. "I promise. But you tell me if it gets more out of hand, okay? If you give me the word, I will get whomever I need to help you."

Leah let go of Sarah, looked down at her hands, and said, "I will. So far, he's only helped when I let him, when I need it. He says he wants Legion just as bad as we do, so I think we use that to our advantage . . . somehow."

"I'm here for you, and I won't say anything, but seriously think about telling someone else, too. Isaac, maybe? I know he has been having a rough time, but he won't betray you. Whatever you do, I trust you."

"Have you seen Isaac? He's barely holding it together. I

can't blame him. None of us are handling this well. But let's keep it between us. For now."

Sarah bit her lip, then nodded. "Of course."

The weight on Leah's chest lightened, and she leaned over and hugged Sarah. "Thank you."

Sarah pulled back and said, "One last thing I think you should know. You might think you are stronger with Asmodeus, but you are the strongest person I've met in my life, even before him. Promise me you won't forget that."

Leah flashed a smile. "I promise."

CHAPTER 5

DREAMER

Leah gazed out the classroom window, watching the rain pattering against the glass for the fifth day in a row. Their missions had all stagnated, but instead of doing nothing, Sid and the others confined the Pawns in a classroom for hours on end. Sid stood at the front of the class, drawing out tactics they'd used on past assignments.

His phone rang, pulling Leah back into the classroom while he picked it up. He looked right at her, nodded, and hung up the phone.

"Pawn Ackerman, Constance wants to see you in her office. We've got a few more runs to go through here, so come back when you're done."

Leah stood and straightened her back, heels together. "Yes, Black Bishop Gunn."

Before leaving, she shot a glance back at Sarah and Isaac who both shrugged in tandem. Constance had barely talked with any of the Pawns for months, let alone summoned one to her office.

Leah found Nykima on the stairs. A quick glance around told her they were alone. She clenched her jaw and hissed, "Why haven't you said anything to him?"

Nykima's gaze hardened. "Watch it, Ackerman."

Leah strained her voice, holding back the anger bubbling up inside her. "It's been months. Brandon still thinks he's out there. How can you think that's okay?"

"Has it occurred to you I'm the one bonded to Roe? I know better than you what's good for him and what information will tip him over the edge. We have more important things going on, Pawn Ackerman, unless you've forgotten that too."

Leah stepped down a stair. The sense of Nykima towering over her was overwhelming. "I can't handle these secrets." Tears streamed down her face as images of Theodore's dead body, killed by her hands, flashed before her. "I have so much guilt. I . . . I can't."

Nykima's gaze softened, and she looked around before leaning in toward Leah. "Listen, you're a fighter. You can carry a burden like this. Brandon is impulsive. I've contained his rage for now, but can you imagine what the news would do to him? He's already a risk with the Tree of Death, and if he learned about his brother before he's ready, it could put him and this entire mission in danger."

"But—"

Nykima rested her hands on Leah's shoulders. "I've been working on our bond, strengthening his connections to the Infinity Board and redirecting his anger. That kind of work takes time and patience. Trust me when I say I am doing everything in my power to help him."

Leah stared into Nykima's eyes, seeing the sincerity as she spoke. She looked away and nodded. "Okay. I trust you."

Nykima let go. "This information is private, understand? You won't mention this again."

Leah's back straightened, and she said, "Understood, White Knight."

Nykima passed by her on the stairs without another word.

Leah reached the ornate wooden doors on the second floor that once led into Dean Wright's office. Now the office belonged to White Bishop Berkenshire. Leah knocked and waited.

"Come in," a voice said from inside the office.

Leah pulled open the doors, stepping inside and standing at attention. "White Bishop Berkenshire. You summoned me?"

Constance sat at the other end of a large mahogany desk covered with stacks of papers and books. The white streak in her otherwise dark black hair had become more prominent in the last few months. She seemed to match the mess in her office, her hair haphazardly tossed up into a bun and her buttoned black and white wool dress stained with what looked like coffee.

She looked at Leah and nodded. "Yes, yes, Pawn Acker-man. Come in and shut the door behind you."

A map of the United States hung on the wall behind Constance, pins holding pictures taken from the rituals in place.

She shuffled around some papers, making a gap for them to see each other. Then she spotted the stack of books on the other chair and pointed. "Hand them here. I'll find a new home for them."

Leah reached down and grabbed the books. The one on top looked like the black leather cover was barely holding it together, and the old gold Hebrew lettering was flaked beyond recognition. She handed the books to Constance, and she piled them behind her, out of sight.

"Apologies for the mess. Research seems to be all I do now. How have you been?" Constance asked as she straightened and buttoned her collar.

Leah sat down in the chair and shrugged. "I'm all right, considering." She restrained herself from returning the question, noting the dark circles under Constance's eyes.

Constance nodded and leaned back in her chair. "I'll cut to the chase, then. We are struggling. Our leads have all but dried up, and the informants we had clearly did not have the information that would get us to the rituals before they happened."

Leah scanned the map behind Constance, noting the dozens of rituals they had found as well as a handful of others they must have been too late for. Images of bodies practically covered the wall, bodies she constantly saw in her head. "So, what does that mean? I'm not ready to give up."

The White Bishop flashed a smirk before staring Leah straight in the eyes. "I was under the impression that you had a skill with dreaming. I seem to recall several instances in your statement after the Wright incident that suggested you could gain intel within your dreams. Intel with a high degree of accuracy. I had hoped you would come to me with more of those dreams, but it seems I need to ask. Have you been dreaming lately?"

A weight settled on Leah's chest. Had Constance been waiting for her this whole time? Was she the reason this team formed in the first place? Was it her fault that they didn't make it on time?

Leah looked down at her fingernails, picking at the sides. "No, I haven't. Not since Dean Wright was killed."

Constance winced at the word. *Killed.* Perhaps Leah could have used a different word. Constance had been bonded to William, and she was the one who executed him when he wouldn't submit. Her face tightened. "Why not? You had plenty before."

Leah's throat went dry. Constance acted like Leah knew

how to use it. "It isn't like a switch. I can't simply turn it on and off. It just happens. Well, at least it used to."

She could make it easy. Just tell Constance that Asmodeus was stopping it, but then what? What would they do to her, to him, to make sure that she could give them what they wanted?

Constance leaned forward and pursed her lips. "That isn't good enough. That skill is rare, but others like you can do it at will. If I knew the practice, I'd train you myself, but—"

"Why don't you get someone else to do it, then? If you know someone else who can, why not them?" Leah couldn't stop herself. The feeling of guilt was heavy on her heart.

"We don't have any other dreamers on the Infinity Board. None. The others who have your skills are no longer interested in dealing with us. They have their own agenda, and we have ours. But we have you. I don't think you understand the severity, but we—"

"Of course I understand. I've seen it myself!" Leah jumped out of her seat.

Constance glared at Leah, standing slowly and shoving her chair out of the way. It rolled with such force that it slammed into her bookshelf, knocking several books free from the wall. She gestured to the map behind her.

"These are all the sacrifices we've found since we formed the Queen's Gambit. I got a call this morning of three others just like them, farther west. Our team has barely been to a quarter of the reported scenes. I only send you out when we have a sliver of hope that we'd make it on time. Your dreams could give us the leverage we need. They are all we have left to stop this bloodshed!"

Leah's cheeks heated, and she clenched her jaw. She couldn't hold back her tongue. "I've been there. I've seen the bodies up close, only minutes after the demons got to them. Where were you?" Leah glared at Constance, seeing her mouth open, but Leah cut her off before she could speak. "You were here, surrounding yourself with books while we feel the pain after every failed job. You think I don't get it? You think I don't want to do everything in my power to stop them? Then, fuck you!"

She turned and stomped toward the door, feeling her fingernails digging into her skin.

"I haven't dismissed you, Pawn Ackerman. Go out that door and you will throw away your chances you have with the Infinity Board. You'll lose any chance of finding answers."

Leah turned and found Constance with her hands behind her back, an eyebrow raised. Constance nodded to the chair and said, "Please sit down. Let us both try to be civil once again."

Leah drew in a deep breath and held it. She could walk out this door, grab her things, and be out of this husk of an academy in minutes. The images on the walls seemed to look back at her, pulling her attention. Families torn apart, all by the hands of the demon who'd ordered Asmodeus to kill her mother.

She let out her breath and went back to the chair, crossing her arms as she sat.

Constance grabbed her chair and sat across from Leah. "I apologize for my outburst. This hunt hasn't been easy for any of us. I've seen nothing like it—the coordination, the speed—and yet, there isn't anything that ties one victim to the other. Nothing. Not even thirty years ago, when Asmodeus tried to bring an army to this side, have we seen something like this."

His name said out loud sent a shiver down Leah's spine. She sat in silence, unsure if Constance wanted her to apologize or what.

Constance started again. "How old are you? Eighteen?"

"Sixteen," Leah corrected.

"So young. I am sorry to put this burden on you, but I'm afraid we have limited options. Queen Helen and I both believe that your dreams could be the key we've been missing. I know you say you can't control it, but could you try? We *must* see Legion's plans well ahead of the informants. It would give us the edge we need."

Leah met Constance's gaze. The woman was beyond tired, and just as broken as everyone else. She needed hope. They all did. "I don't know how to do it. But I will do everything I can to see if I can make it happen."

A smile grew across Constance's face. "That's all I ask."

CHAPTER 6
A DARK ALLY

Leah lay awake in her bed, staring at the ceiling as the moon rose and traced across the otherwise darkened room. Falling asleep was easy when she wanted to, but trying to dream was like climbing a mountain in scuba gear.

She had to make herself dream, though. Had to figure out what the demons were up to, what their next move was. She squeezed her eyes shut, hearing Constance's voice echoing in her head, telling her that her dreams were the key and how she could stop the bloodshed.

Taking in another slow breath, she pushed out Constance's voice and focused on Legion. She wondered where he was, where he would be. The map behind Constance surfaced in her mind, clear as day, smoke billowing off the edges. All the pins and pictures appeared, seemingly in the exact spot she remembered seeing them.

It was odd to see places they hadn't even been to, including New York, Texas, and even Northern California, clustered with pins. Could they have saved the victims if the Queen's Gambit knew about these places? The other pins were places she remembered, each one that surrounded North Carolina, all the way up to Pennsylvania, over to Kansas, and back south to Florida. Nearly all those faces were familiar.

The pins were all black. Leah racked her mind, trying to remember the board she'd seen when she was awake. The pins weren't all black in the waking world. As if responding to that thought, the pins shifted and changed colors. Red pins surfaced around California, and blue started around North Carolina. Each color spread across the map, some pins turning, others staying black.

Leah brought her mind closer to the map, eyeing the red and wondering if what she saw was a pattern.

Pain shot through her head, a piercing agony that felt like she'd split her skull in half. The map vanished, and she lurched up.

She'd expected to be lying in bed. Instead, she stood in ankle deep waters of an endless black ocean.

"I told you not to do that," Asmodeus's weak voice echoed from somewhere distant.

"Was that you?" Leah shouted, holding her hand to her head, wincing from the dulled pain.

"I told you not to try until we were ready. I'd been storing away energy to prepare. Instead, I've had to use some on you."

She glared at him. Her stomach turned over, fear bubbling to the surface. If he could stop her like that, what else could he do? She pushed the thought down with her fear, not willing to let Asmodeus see. "I got the message loud and clear. Can we talk now, please?"

"There is nothing to talk about, not yet." His voice grew farther away.

Leah took a step forward, unsure if it moved her any closer to him. "Wait! Please. I just want to understand. I want to listen this time, I swear."

After a long moment of silence, the demon's voice echoed back, "All right."

The same white table manifested in front of her, unbroken, and a chair materialized behind her. When she sat, Asmodeus appeared on the other side of the table dressed in the same black suit, but now appearing more emaciated than normal. His eyes looked more like hollow sockets, and his neck was nearly swallowed up by the collar of his suit, which hung off him as if it were several sizes too big.

He folded his hands together. "So, are you ready to have a civilized conversation?"

The pain still ached in Leah's skull. "Why did you do that?"

"Whatever it was you were doing, you were reaching out into the Astral, making yourself visible to anyone looking. Legion is looking for you. It was only a matter of time before he found you. So, I stopped it."

"We need to know where he is. We need to stop him. Everyone else in the Queen's Gambit is out of options."

Asmodeus let in a slow, wheezy breath before speaking. "There aren't many of your kind. Constance called it dreaming, yes? We demons call them Watchers, but still the same."

Leah leaned forward, her eyes widening. "My kind? What does that mean?"

Asmodeus grinned. "You humans have many ways to connect to your Trees, but Mystics and Watchers have the born talents that others do not. A Mystic's abilities protect the material world, while a Watcher's abilities are more focused on protecting the Astral. Watchers are such a nuisance when trying to cross over. And you seem to have potential for that since you can travel into the Astral without a ritual. However, without control, you are a beacon, and an open invitation to anyone looking."

"So, splitting my skull open is your way of telling me to back off?"

Asmodeus nodded. "Pain without injury, if you are at all concerned. But Legion knows what you are now, which means he knows how to trap you."

Leah kicked back the chair and stood. "I need to find him! We need his next move. They're relying on me to get it."

Asmodeus let out a raspy laugh that echoed into the surrounding nothingness.

"What's so funny?" Leah asked, crossing her arms.

"You and your kind won't ever stop amusing me. I warn you that Legion is waiting to trap you, and you persist and put yourself at risk for others. Why? Why do you care so much?"

Acid rose in her throat, and she squeezed her arms tighter to her body. Still, the words came out smoother and more controlled than she thought. "Because of you. Because of what you did to my family. I don't want that to happen to anyone else again. I'm a Mystic. A protector. If my sacrifice means fewer people have to go through what I've been through, then so be it."

Asmodeus's smile fell as she talked, and he remained quiet for a long time. When he finally spoke, it held the same sincerity in Leah's voice. "That is very noble of you. I think we may have more in common than you think, even though I was the hand that caused you so much sorrow. Please, listen to me when I say this; we have an opportunity to work together to beat Legion. The more we learn, the stronger we will become. As you grow into the Tree of Life, I can continue to study and pull on the Tree of Death through you and cleanse it from the corruption. Your sacrifice now would be for nothing, a waste of energy, and a waste of resources."

Leah placed her hands on her hips. "I'm sorry? What have you been doing with the Tree of Death?"

Asmodeus let out a slight smirk. "Did you really not know? Did you think Invisibility was just another well no one told you about?"

Leah took a step back. "That was . . . you? That was the Tree of Death?"

He nodded. "We demons need energy—life—to survive. The easiest thing to do is feed off the host and take over their body. However, I've found that the corruptive force, the energy that would otherwise drive you mad, has been quite palatable. Something I've never been able to do before. Atop that, it has granted you access to something others dare not try."

"Why not just take over my body? You *are* a demon, after all."

"Don't think I didn't want to. But I barely had enough essence to latch on to your mark and save myself from Legion."

Leah felt her heart leap in her chest. He would have possessed her if he could? At least he was honest. "So, Invisibility is part of the Tree of Death?"

Asmodeus let out another chuckle. "Your people call it *Thagirion*. It opposes *Tiferet* on your Trees. The one you know sees beyond what you can normally perceive, and the other conceals what is already perceivable."

Leah dropped her gaze, remembering how it felt to call on *Thagirion* and the odd feeling it gave her. She should have felt shame or fear. Instead, she knew the advantages it gave her. How it helped her save Joanna in the bathroom. Or how Asmodeus had taken over and used it to protect her. Was it wrong to want this power?

"Don't feel shame or fear. You and I could have everything we need to defeat Legion. We can save your people and mine."

His words caught her off guard. She looked up at him, spotting the distant look in his eye. "Your people? You mean other demons?"

"People of The Valley, my home. Not all of us want to be enslaved by that tyrant. We just want to live and save our home from his hand."

"Wait, what do you know about Legion?"

Asmodeus stood, and as he did, the table vanished and the black sea of water turned into red sand. Hot air blew through Leah's hair, and fragrances she couldn't quite put her finger on blew by.

"I've known him longer than you can even imagine, well before our world fell into a desolation that consumed so many of my kind. He is chaos incarnate and will stop at nothing to get what he wants."

The sand receded back into the waters, and the hot air shifted to cold. Asmodeus turned his back to Leah. "I still need more time to prepare. You and I will have our revenge. Soon."

Leah stepped forward, reaching for his arm. "Wait, but what about Legion? What can he do? How can we stop him? What about the other de—"

Her hand passed through his arm, and he vanished, leaving Leah alone in the dark and endless sea.

CHAPTER 7
INFORMANTS

Leah spooned her cup of yogurt, tasting the slight metallic flavor of artificial sweetener mixed with strawberry. The little cups of yogurt, fruit, and granola sat at the end of what used to be a buffet line, once used to feed more than a hundred people. Now, it was an anomaly if all thirteen members of the Queen's Gambit and the guards were in the space at the same time. And that was without counting Queen Helen, technically the fourteenth member, who rarely showed up at the academy.

Exhaustion loomed over Leah, covering her like a weighted blanket. Her conversation with Asmodeus had taken a toll on her sleep for the rest of the night. He didn't really tell her anything useful, and he was keeping her a prisoner in her own mind.

She looked up from her plastic cup, across the room toward another table. Sid, Nykima, and Eric sat there pointing and whispering over stacks of papers and unfolded maps.

Would her uncle flip out if he knew about Asmodeus? Sarah hadn't; she'd taken it better than Leah had thought she would. Maybe he would be the same, and she'd be able to get some advice on what to do.

"Earth to Leah, you there?" Isaac asked, waving his hand in front of her face.

Leah shook her head and blinked a few times before yawning. "Yeah, sorry. Rough night."

Sarah downed the last of her orange juice and eyed Leah. "You sure it's nothing else?"

Isaac looked over at Sarah, raised an eyebrow, and then looked back at Leah. "What's this about? You two better not be fighting again."

Sarah let out a snort and shoved Isaac's shoulder. "No, you dork. It's nothing. Stop overthinking."

Leah pushed her food away and let out a big overhead stretch before saying, "It's not that. I'll . . . tell you later. Okay?"

Gabe plopped into the seat next to Isaac and let out an enormous sigh.

"What is it now, lover boy?" Sarah asked.

Gabe hovered over his food, peeling back his yogurt. "Nothing."

Leah looked over Gabe's shoulder and spotted Joanna. She sat at a table full of guards, laughing. "Doesn't look like nothing."

The overhead speakers crackled to life, echoing throughout the academy. "Meeting, Room One, Five Minutes."

Sarah cradled her head in her hands and sighed. "I'm not ready for another mission. Not yet."

Isaac stood and grabbed the remains of his breakfast. "Let's just get it over with. After, maybe I'll have you steal a laptop and bring it over to the nook. I'm pretty sure I can get it past the firewall and stream movies."

Sarah's eyes lit up. "A petty theft and movies?" She

hopped up out of her seat and smiled. "I'm in! But the computers in the offices are way better than the old trash they keep in the library."

Isaac gave Sarah a devilish smile. "Oh, I know."

Leah waited for Gabe to get up, and they followed Sarah and Isaac as they left the cafeteria and found seats in the classroom. Eric, Sid, and Nykima took up spots in the front row, while they took seats in the third. Shortly after them, the other Pawns filtered in, joining them in the second and third rows.

Constance and Grace stepped into the room, and everyone leaped out of their seats to stand at attention.

"At ease. Take a seat," Constance said, holding her hands behind her back in front of the chalkboard. Grace, the second in command, stood near the door.

Constance waited for the others to sit before starting. "Good morning, everyone. As you would have already guessed, we have new orders." She traced her eyes across the room, stopping a moment longer at Leah's before continuing. "I've been talking with Queen Helen, and our tactics have been unsuccessful. I am aware of the impact it has had on all of you. Because of that, the Infinity Board has agreed to change our approach."

Constance took a step back and nodded at Grace.

Grace stepped forward. "Informants have given Queen Helen the time and locations of the next four sacrifices. Our enemy is still unknown. The informants are still getting their information three or four times removed from the source. We don't know their numbers. Our orders are to get intel. Any bit of information we can get will help."

Constance nodded at Grace and looked out at the others. "I will assign each Knight and Bishop one of these jobs with their collective charges. This order is for intel only. The Infinity Board has instructed us to not intervene, hence why we are splitting into your core squads to cover more ground. Sneak in undetected and get an eye on the enemy."

Sid raised a finger and cleared his throat. "And what of the sacrifices?"

Constance nodded. "The orders are explicit. Those sacrificed during these assignments will not be in vain. Their deaths will provide valuable information for our mission."

Leah's stomach churned. She stood, glaring down at Constance. "You want us to watch someone get murdered and do nothing? After everything we've been trying to do? What's wrong with you?"

"Leah! Enough!" Eric said, turning and glaring at her. His surprise and outrage traveled through the bond, mixing and echoing against her own frustration.

"No! We've been at this for months with nothing to show. This is backwards. It's wrong."

Constance adjusted her stance and raised her eyebrows. "Do you have a way to gather more accurate information from our enemy that you'd like to share?" She paused for a moment, waiting for an answer Leah didn't have. "No? Then this is the best option the Infinity Board has. Unless you have grown fond of arriving late and seeing the carnage."

Leah couldn't let this go. She knew what Constance meant, that it was this or Leah's dreams, and she couldn't give Constance what she wanted. "We sacrifice ourselves for the greater good. We protect others when they need it most. How do you expect us to just sit in silence while these people get executed?"

Leah felt the energy inside her uncoil and press up against her skin. The tension in the room grew thick.

Calm yourself, Asmodeus said in her mind.

Leah let in a slow breath and did everything in her power to keep from making it worse.

Constance waited for Leah to relax. She looked at Eric, who nodded before she started again. "In times of war, the sacrifice of some may cause a turning of the tides. We are gaining no ground as it is, so this is the Infinity Board's best approach with the resources at hand. A mere White Pawn shouldn't be questioning that. You've had your outburst. One more word out of your mouth, and you will face discipline. Understood? Now, sit down."

A lump formed in Leah's throat. She studied the room, searching for any sign of fight in anyone else's eyes, but they all looked away.

Leah's hands grew cold and sweaty, and she stumbled back into her seat, her eyes locked on the desk in front of her.

Leah didn't talk to anyone while the Pawns walked to the second classroom. After the academy had closed, they'd stocked the second classroom with guns, weapons, and gear, converting it into a makeshift armory. Leah tightened her bulletproof vest, holstered her gun, and checked her knives before sitting down at the end of the bench near the window.

Lost in thought, she didn't notice when someone rested their hand on her shoulder until they shook her. She turned, seeing Gabe looking down at her. "Hey, the others are all out in the hall if you want to join us."

She shrugged him off and looked back out the window. "No, I think I'm good here."

He paused, then said, "You know, you weren't wrong."

"Then why didn't you say anything? Why didn't any of you?"

He let out a sigh. "I don't know. It didn't feel like my place to speak up. The Infinity Board knows what they're doing. It's not like we've had a ton of luck out there."

Leah shook her head. "But this? You're telling me they couldn't come up with something else? Anything else? And you all just accept it?"

Gabe took a step back. "What else are we supposed to do? We're Pawns. If we want to make a difference, we follow orders and wait until we have the authority to decide."

"Or tear it all down and start over," Leah mumbled.

"Saying that is going to get you in trouble."

Cold sweat formed on her brow, and she wiped it away as she stood. "You're right. I just want something better. But we've got to do this, I know."

She followed him out into the lobby, catching the wary eyes of Sarah and Isaac before giving them a half smile.

"You ready for this?" Isaac asked.

Leah shrugged. "It's not like I have much of a choice. You?"

Isaac mimicked Leah. "Yeah, I guess."

Gabe stared at the ceiling, choosing his words slowly, "Your bravery never fails to surprise me. I used to think I was just another pawn in the Infinity Board's game, but your unwillingness to accept your place is both dangerous and inspiring."

"You could say that again," Sarah interjected, nudging Leah's side.

Eric and the others stepped out of the classroom. Constance eyed Leah before saying, "Best of luck to all of you." Then she turned and headed up the stairs to her office.

Sid walked over to Gabe and smacked him gently on the shoulder before looking over at Isaac and Ricardo. "You three ready to go?"

Isaac perked up, his face flushing white. "Wait. Bathroom." He raced off.

Sid shook his head. "That kid kills me. Anyone else? You've all got a long trip ahead. Best to go now."

Grace straightened her vest. "Team, form up!"

Sarah shot Leah a look before diving in for a quick hug. "Don't do anything stupid."

Leah attempted to glare while suppressing a smile. "Thanks. You too."

Sarah raced to Grace's side while Joanna took her time.

Eric stood beside Leah and rocked on his heels. "You all ready?"

"Yeah," Leah said, not quite ready to look him in the eyes.

They walked out the large doors, and as they stepped down the marbled steps, Eric leaned toward Leah and said in a low voice, "For what it's worth, I don't like this too much either."

CHAPTER 8
MEMORIES

Leah stared out the window while Eric weaved through the narrow roads of the Nantahala National Forest. They'd been like this for hours, Leah pretending she wasn't there.

Eric tightened his grip on the steering wheel and cleared his throat. "You know what you did back there was wrong, right? Talking out of line to a superior."

"Someone had to say something."

Eric didn't reply right away. He shifted in his seat and sighed. "You remind me of her so much."

Leah felt a cluster of emotions travel through the bond, one after the other. Happiness, guilt, sadness, and grief. Her eyes watered uncontrollably. "Who?"

"Your mother." He paused, waiting for Leah to reply. When none didn't come, he continued. "Not just the looks, but your actions. She was so impulsive, even when I was at the academy and she was a White Pawn. Never afraid to speak her mind."

Warmth rose in her chest, a soothing sensation she wanted to keep hold of forever. "What was she like? In the Infinity Board?"

Eric gave a halfhearted smirk. "Lizzy was amazing. Everything I aspired to be. Brave and strong, first to enter a burning building and make sure everyone made it out alive. She was loyal too. She and the Black Queen were forces to be reckoned with."

Leah's breath caught in her chest, remembering the photo of the two as young Pawns. "I saw a photo of them in the same class at the academy."

Eric laughed. "They were inseparable. Best Pawns in their class and quickest to be promoted to Black Knights. Later, they defeated Asmodeus when he was at the peak of his power. They were superstars of their time."

A surge of pain leaped up her arm, and a hiss sounded in the back of her mind. Leah jumped.

Eric shot her a glance. "What the hell was that?"

"Nothing." She rubbed at her arm and shook her head. "It's just . . . I didn't know all this about her."

He took in a breath and chewed his bottom lip. "I know. Your mom quit after the encounter with Asmodeus. She was barely in her twenties, but they wanted to promote her to Black Rook and bring her onto the outer council. She would have been a great leader. They even offered her a role as a sage, but she just quit, and the Board struck her from the record like they do with anyone who leaves."

Leah looked down at her boots and picked at her fingernails. "But why did she leave? The fight was over. At least, the war with Asmodeus."

"War, yeah, but things didn't change much. Demons kept coming, and the world needed protecting. I was just getting promoted to White Pawn, after finishing my training at the Academy, when she showed up. Her eyes were . . . different. She came to say goodbye, and there was nothing I could do or say to stop her from leaving."

Leah kept her head down, her mind racing with what her mother must have gone through to make that decision.

"From war hero to a deserter in a matter of weeks." Eric shrugged. "But that's the Board's way. When you commit to something like protecting humanity and seeking knowledge, turning away from that makes you out to be the bad guy."

"That's not fair," Leah mumbled.

"It's not, but she knew that. Whatever part of her that was keeping her in the Infinity Board died when she defeated Asmodeus. I figured I'd never see her smile again. It took years, but it happened."

"When?"

"The day you were born," Eric said, beaming. "They couldn't keep me from her, being family and all, so I got to see when her fighting spirit came back. The same one I see in you. And the same one that Constance sees in both of you."

Leah scoffed. "Why'd you have to ruin it by bringing her up?"

"Because you butting heads with her won't help anyone."

"But she's insane, ordering us to do this. She can't expect us to just sit there and watch someone die. I don't think any of us can take that. I know I can't."

Eric sighed and tapped his hands on the wheel. "And you really think that's what she wants?"

"That's what she ordered us to do. You were there. Are you telling me you heard nothing she said?"

"White Bishop Berkenshire simply stated what her superiors believe is the best approach. She has to follow a chain of command as much as we do. On top of that, she can't stand up and argue against them as much as a White Pawn shouldn't be standing up against their superiors."

Leah ignored that last comment. "What's that mean, though? She doesn't want us to follow orders?"

Eric shook his head. "We get the intel. That *is* the order. My guess is that whomever on the council made the order knows we need to split up. And if we put ourselves in danger on their orders, it'll look bad on them. So, they're instructing us to not intervene."

Leah tilted her head. "So, what, do you think she was telling us to intervene? That's not what I heard."

"Well, she doesn't want us to get hurt, either. What I do know is that it was enough to rile you up. Enough to get you to say the things she couldn't. Which might make us all more willing to intervene if we have the numbers to do so."

"So, she used me?"

Eric turned off the highway. "Starting to catch on? Wouldn't you say it was strange that speaking to a superior officer only got you a slap on the wrists? Any other White Bishop would have placed you under disciplinary confinement for your insubordination. I've seen it done for far less than what you did."

Leah grimaced and felt bile rise in her throat. She'd been used again and didn't even know that she had fallen right into Constance's game. It made her sick.

She pushed the feeling down and looked out the window, focusing on the trees passing by. After a moment, she asked, "So, where are we going?"

"A secluded part of Chattahoochee National Forest, in Georgia. Still have an hour to go."

She waited a little longer, chewing at her lip, before turning and asking, "Are we going to save them? If we get the chance?"

Eric looked over and raised an eyebrow. "You really *are* something."

"Why do you say that?"

"You don't just remind me of Lizzy. You've got some Jade in you too." His voice cracked, and he swallowed hard.

Leah's raised an eyebrow. "Your other Pawn, right? Before me?"

He nodded. "I had just been promoted to Black Knight and headed up to an academy in New York. She was as much a fighter as you and your mother."

"Hotheaded and stubborn?"

Eric laughed. "A bit of that. But mostly courageous and brave, like you. One time, some guards caught her friend sneaking food out from the cafeteria. She was there too but got away. She went back, though, and took the punishment with him—a hundred laps around the training court. Even helped him up when he fell more than once. I was out back having a smoke when they finished. After hours of punishment, they were still sneaking food out. I figured they were just being stupid teenagers. I followed them about a half mile down the road, to a women's shelter. That's when I found out what they were really doing with the food." Eric slowed the car and turned down a dirt road. "I knew I'd made the right choice, bonding with her. We were a formidable team. We took down a cult in Boston by ourselves the first year. The Board started sending us across the country. I couldn't tell you how many demons we exorcised. We were good. *She* was good." He tightened his grip on the steering wheel, his knuckles turning white.

Leah shifted in her seat. "What happened?"

"We were on assignment out in California. We'd just come from a long mission working with a community of Druids. I guess we were both a little cocky. Intel said there was an entity causing trouble at a Rehab Center, but it turned out to be a third level demon. It wasn't alone either. By the time I realized what we were facing, it was too late. They ambushed us. Possessed everyone in the building too.

We were cornered, and it wasn't looking good. Then Jade called on the Tree of Death. She saved me, but I couldn't stop her. The Tree overtook her, and there was nothing I could do."

Pain surged through the bond, and Leah felt tears fall from her face. "I'm sorry."

He slowed the car and looked out the side window. "Worst day of my life was seeing the faces of her parents. I wanted . . . no, I *needed* them to know. I had to apologize for what happened, but I couldn't bring myself to tell them what happened to their daughter. I'm a coward." Eric fished around in his pocket for a moment, sighed, then returned his empty hand to the wheel.

Leah grabbed his shoulder and squeezed. "You're not a coward. You fight on for her. You keep her alive that way. If it were me instead of Jade, and you kept fighting for me, that would be more than enough."

Eric's lips curved into a small, sad smile. He parked the car and sat, staring out at the leaves swaying back and forth in the trees. He wiped his eyes and checked his side before saying, "We're here," and opening the car door.

CHAPTER 9

THE RITUAL

Eric opened the trunk, pulling out the camera and a pair of binoculars. "Stay close and ready your gun, just in case. We've got another mile on foot."

They hiked through dense forest, the humid air sticking to Leah's skin as she held on tight to her gun. Had she been visiting for any other reason, Leah would have taken in the rolling hills or the occasional waterfall. Instead, she scanned every inch of the land in front of her, vigilant for any signs of movement.

Once they reached the summit of a hill overlooking a valley, Eric raised a fist and they paused. He looked around, then signaled for them to crouch down in place. He turned back to her, his eyes glowing yellow, and waved for Leah to join behind him as he crawled into some bushes.

She took out her binoculars to follow his line of sight, but the foliage was too dense. Leah closed her eyes and wakened the heaviness in her chest. It moved up her neck and into her head, a pressure that made her ears pop. Warmth built behind her eyes, and when she opened them, the world around her brightened.

She could see individual veins of leaves twenty feet

away, ants marching past her and into an anthill off in the brush, a fox racing between them, and a collection of glowing silhouettes off in the distance.

Her focus shifted to them, and she spotted two targets two hundred yards away. They glowed with a speckled yellow light, evidence that demons tainted the energy. She blinked a few times as she let go of *Tiferet* and waited for her normal vision to come back.

The world around her looked diluted, and her vision blurred around the edges, but she looked at Eric.

"You spotted them, right?" Eric whispered to her.

"Yeah, two up ahead. Camouflaged."

Eric nodded and spun his finger in a circle in the air. "Let's circle around them. I need a better angle. On my six."

Leah followed Eric as they crept in a wide circle around the location of the two demons. Her knees and back ached from the crouching as they reached their last vantage point. She fell into the base of a tree and gathered her bearings as Eric scanned the area.

She could see clearly through the brush from this point without relying on *Tiferet*. The two whom they had identified were a tall Black man and a muscular woman who looked to be of Indian descent.

Eric unzipped his pack and retrieved the camera, aiming it at the two and pressing the record button before panning past them and to the clearing behind them.

It looked like other clearings they had come across before, with a single tree near the middle.

"Why are they just standing there?" she whispered to Eric.

"They're possessed. My guess is they're being ordered to stand guard by a higher-level demon."

The two demons stood inhumanly still, staring out into nothingness while Leah and Eric waited. The sun trailed across the sky, and from time to time, Leah used *Tiferet* to scan the area.

By the time the sun reached the horizon, Eric nudged her and nodded off to the east. "They're coming."

Leah's eyes glowed again, but she couldn't see anything other than the two silhouettes in front of her. "Where?"

"Ten o'clock. Still far off."

Leah scanned the area, but nothing came into view. Her skill with *Tiferet* was good, but she hadn't realized until now how much ability she lacked with the other abilities of the Tree of Life.

Eric pulled out the camera and set it up, while Leah switched to binoculars and waited, using the last bits of light to track their movement. Three people came into view, two on either side of a man wrapped in chains that forced him to hunch over and waddle as the other two pulled him by a thick collar around his neck. She focused on the man's face and spotted the horns protruding out of his head, curling down. His beard and chest hair were thick and wiry, but the scars and cuts that covered his body still shone through.

Eric cocked his head, grabbing his binoculars for confirmation. "Is that a—"

"Chimera," Leah finished, chills racing down her back.

The demon on the right, a middle-aged balding man, held the end of the chain that was wrapped around the chimera's collar and constantly hit him with a rod, but the chimera wasn't resisting. In fact, he barely even flinched, keeping in line with his escorts.

They reached the clearing, and the two demons who stood like statues came to life and helped restrain the chimera against a tree.

"Chimeras are supposed to be working with Legion,"

Eric said, zooming in on the bizarre scene. "I don't understand. Why are they sacrificing him?"

Every sacrifice they'd been to, every picture on Constance's wall was a human. Yet Leah stared at the chimera as they tightened his restraints. "Maybe they're getting desperate?"

They watched as the four demons circled around the tree, joining hands and swaying side to side.

The chimera lolled his head upward to the sky, struggling against some unseen force before dropping his head down to his chest.

"They drugged him," Eric said, grabbing onto the camera and focusing it on him. "So, maybe the chimeras aren't working with them. This one isn't, at least."

The four hummed a discordant melody, one that made the hairs on Leah's arm stand on end. They let go of each other and began undulating their bodies, dancing to some unheard beat. Their arms flailed inward, toward the chimera, then shook violently to the sky. The humming turned into words, a language that brought a buzz to her arm and a sense of familiarity and longing.

Her arm twitched and moved of its own accord, reaching out to them.

The Black man, whose back faced Leah and Eric, froze. Then, with a loud crack, his neck snapped backward and his face peered out into the bushes toward their location.

She could see the whites of his eyes, like two poached eggs, staring back at her. She pulled back on her arm, cradling it close to her, and the sense of longing vanished. A moment later, he stood back up and carried on with the dance as if nothing had happened.

The song stopped, and the four raised their hands to the darkening sky, cracking and popping their necks backward. The Indian woman pulled a silver blade from her side and pointed it to the sky, belting out a scream that the others echoed. She squeezed tight on the hilt of the dagger, aiming the point down, right at the chimera.

"We have to do something," Leah muttered.

"Whatever you are scheming, don't. We can't take on four of them without—"

The dagger descended toward the chimera's chest, and time seemed to slow down. Leah stood up from the bushes, her eyes trained on the demons. She couldn't sit still. She couldn't let another person be sacrificed. Energy rippled down her arms.

She clapped her hands together, and a bubble of energy billowed out of her toward her targets.

It flew past the Demons in an instant, and their movements immediately halted. Leah had completely frozen them in a field of *Hod*.

Eric shot up. "What the hell are you doing?"

Leah's hands jerked, and the sound of breaking glass shattered in her ear. Each of the demons shook in tandem, and the dagger got closer to the chimera. They fought against her hold, aiming to finish their ritual.

"I can't hold them."

"God dammit!" Eric shouted. "Be ready to get in the fight and have my back. *Malchut* to the head if you can."

Glass cracked again in her ear, and a force pressed against her hands as if trying to rip them apart.

Eric crossed the clearing in an instant, using *Malchut* to boost him, landing in front of the woman with the dagger. He reeled his hand back and connected, open palm, with the side of her head.

Leah's *Hod* shattered as the woman went flying and crashed into a tree. She fell limp as the other demons shook their bodies and turned to Eric.

They all flanked him.

Leah forced *Malchut* into her feet and leaped off the ground.

She landed behind the Black man and swiped her leg underneath him. He twisted and fell. Before he hit the ground, he caught himself on all fours, like some animal. He jerked his head up to Leah and screamed before jumping at her.

She punched his side midair, her attack enhanced with *Malchut* launching him off course and tumbling yards away toward the edge of the clearing.

Kill them, Asmodeus said.

"What? No," Leah said under her breath.

The demon raced toward her again, and her left arm moved against her will. Asmodeus pulled on *Nehemoth* as the demon lunged at her, hastening its speed.

She dove out of the way. The demon moved too fast and crashed headfirst into a tree, sending bark flying in all directions. The demon swayed to his feet and looked at Leah. A massive gash split his forehead, and blood covered his face.

Her left hand twitched again, and Leah grabbed it. "Stop it! You're not helping!"

They have to die. They won't stop.

The demon raced after her. She pushed her left arm out of the way, and with her right gave the demon a *Malchut*-enhanced uppercut. He lifted off the ground several feet before crumpling to the ground, unconscious.

Kill him.

Leah turned and saw Eric down on one knee as the two demons clawed and scratched at his face. Their fingers slid off him, leaving him completely unblemished from the assault. *Netzach*, the Invulnerable. One of them, a long-haired blond, a skinny kid only a few years older than her, leaped toward Leah. Blood covered his mangled fingertips, each with razor-sharp bones protruding from them.

He swiped at her, his clawed hands barely grazing her, but they sliced through her shirt and cut into her side.

Leah jumped back, feeling the sting, and pulled on the energy of *Netzach*, allowing it to cover her like armor. With it came the addictive feeling. The sense that she could do anything.

She jumped forward without a care that his fingers were mere inches from her face. They glided off like raindrops on a windshield. She opened her palm and slammed it into the side of his head. He tumbled through the air before digging his boney claws into the ground.

The demon who'd been attacking the chimera landed next to Leah and grabbed her ankles.

She slipped, pulled to the ground by the demon who climbed on top of her and screamed.

Kill him! Asmodeus shouted.

The demon clawed at her, fingertips sliding off. Pressure built in her chest, and she let *Malchut* pulse out, throwing the demon off. She pushed up to her feet and launched off the ground, fist connecting with the middle-aged man and knocking him unconscious.

She turned, ready to see the blond-haired demon readying himself for another attack, but his body lay on the ground next to Eric.

"We got them," she said, panting.

"We did. But how about we don't . . ." Eric's eyes widened, and he pointed behind her. "Leah! Look out!"

Leah turned and saw the Indian woman barreling toward her, dagger in hand, and closing in. She lifted her arm and sliced through the air, a move that felt all too natural to her.

A thin stream of *Malchut* flew, slicing into the woman's midsection.

The woman froze, looked down, then choked as blood poured from her waist. She fell to her knees, dropping the dagger. She looked up at Leah, her eyes no longer enraged like some deranged killer, but eyes filled with tears. "Where? What happened?"

Leah stepped back, *Tiferet* filling her eyes. The black flecks she expected to see were gone, and she only saw a dimming golden light.

"I . . . I'm sorry." Leah couldn't find any other words as she watched the woman look to her waist, then to the trees.

"My son. Have you seen my son? He needs his teddy, otherwise he won't . . . he won't nap."

The woman fell to the ground, life leaving her eyes.

Leah slumped down, her hand reaching out.

Eric grabbed her shoulder. "Come on. We need to get out of here before they wake up."

"But I . . . I killed her."

Eric pulled her to her feet. He rested his hands on her shoulders and closed his eyes. He took in a sharp breath, and the pain Leah had been feeling seemed to numb. "You did. But it was either her or you. If we don't get out of here now, then we're going to have to take care of the others. Do you want that?"

She shook her head as her eyes watered, and her jaw shook.

"Okay, then grab the camera and help me get the chimera off the tree."

CHAPTER 10

AFTERSHOCK

Leah helped Eric drag the unconscious chimera back into the car and slowly placed him in the back seat, tying his hands together with fluorescent orange tow straps. When she climbed into the front passenger seat, Leah realized she was shaking. The woman's death replayed over and over in her mind, and her words wouldn't stop echoing.

My son. Have you seen my son?

Eric started the engine and backed out of the parking spot, speeding away and onto the road. After a few minutes of silence, he reached out and grabbed Leah's hand. "Hey, listen to me. Keep yourself together, okay? You saved the chimera. Remember that."

Leah shook her head, looking out the window at the trees passing by. "Her son won't see his mom again. I . . . I killed her." Another wave of numbness washed over her, dulling her senses.

Eric squeezed her hand, then let go and held on tight to the steering wheel, wincing. "I know. I know. I can't say much that will make it feel better. Please, if you can, just focus on the bond. Focus on me."

She took in a few deep breaths, imagining the connection between her and Eric. She felt his calm wash over her. "I just . . . how are you so calm?" She lost the connection between them, instead feeling *Malchut* unwind in her chest. "She's dead. Theodore's dead. Alma's dead. They're all dead. If I wasn't here . . . if I didn't . . ."

"Focus on me Leah. Breathe. What's done is done. The moment you think of what could have been will be the moment you lose yourself."

Leah looked down at her hands and shook her head. "But this. Do I even want this? It's wrong. We *kill* people."

"We do everything we can to mitigate loss, but there will be death along the way. Can't stop it. Not unless there was some magic wand that could give demons what they wanted without the expense of a person."

He's right, Asmodeus said. *There's no use crying now.*

"Shut up!" Leah shouted, slamming her fists onto her knees.

Eric swayed the car from the sudden outburst and frowned, keeping his eyes on the road.

"I didn't mean it," Leah said. "I'm sorry."

"Yes, you did mean it," Eric said. "And that's okay. I can't tell you how to feel. Even with the *Yesod* bond, I can't read all your emotions. I thought I could with Jade, and we know where that ended up."

Leah looked at the road ahead and sighed. "How did you handle it your first time?"

"Handle what?"

"You know," Leah said. "Killing someone."

"I was fourteen," Eric started. "Youngest of my outpost. It was during the war with Asmodeus. Corruption infiltrated the Infinity Board and compromised our outpost, among others. We were lucky. Had enough time to get out in the dead of night. I got lost, tripping over a root in the woods. A woman showed up. She was nice. Helped me to my feet and asked if I was okay. I was stupid, and the idea of demons was just so new to me. I figured she was the rescue party."

Leah bit her lip. "But . . . she wasn't."

Eric shook his head. "Far from it. One of the other Squares, Kenny Brok, turned back to get me. Shouted for me to get away. We were good friends. She killed him before I processed what was happening. She looked at me, blood all over her face. *Malchut* came out of me so fast that it sent her right through a tree branch like a pincushion."

"But she was going to attack you," Leah said. "She would have killed you."

"And that woman back there was about to do the same."

The realization hit Leah like a ton of bricks. Her uncle was right. Still, that voice wouldn't stop echoing in her head.

Leah watched the trees slowly transition into homes and then homes give way to the highway. The numbness inside her lessened, and the pain it subdued seemed less. She picked at her fingers, reliving the moment in her head.

"I just I don't think I can let it go."

"And I'm not saying you should. It's hard. It's always hard. You, me . . . hell, Jade even. We all had to face the fact that this duty of ours is not pretty. You've seen it firsthand. Seen what carnage they can do."

"But are we right? If we can just kill people and argue that we're protecting them. Is that supposed to be okay?"

Eric relaxed in his seat and ran a hand through his hair. "We limit the damage, but there will always be loss. Collateral damage. If we did nothing, then demons would continue to spread. They'd keep killing and taking away the lives we hold dear. We can't forget the ones we've lost along the way, but we have to move on for a greater cause."

"And you truly believe that?" Leah asked.

"I do. I have to. Otherwise, everything I've done—everything Lizzy did, everything Jade did—it's all for nothing. I refuse to believe that. I refuse to think that we aren't making an impact and that we aren't shielding the people from something far worse than they could ever imagine. The rest of the world will never know it, but we protect them because we are Mystics."

Leah turned and looked in the back seat, back at the unconscious chimera. "I saved him. I suppose that has to stand for something, right?"

CHAPTER II

INSUBORDINATION

"You two disobeyed a direct order." Constance pursed her lips, standing behind her desk.

Leah picked at her fingers, the dead woman's face still burning in her mind.

Eric stepped forward. "We saw an opportunity, White Bishop."

"And what made you think there was an opportunity to be had? This was a recon mission, and you were only supposed to be gathering information."

"We saw enough. This was our best chance to capture a chimera, alive, and question it."

"And you think that *thing* will give us answers, Black Knight?" Constance asked, stepping out from behind her desk and closing in on Eric.

Eric clenched his jaw but stood firm. "We saved his life."

Constance pointed her finger at Eric. "And how do you know that monster wanted to be saved? How do you know you didn't just bring a spy into our headquarters?"

Every moment, Leah wanted to cut off Constance and

intervene, but a weight held her down. The woman in the woods still stared back at her with dead eyes. No matter how much numbing Eric tried to give her through the *Yesod* bond, she couldn't let go of what she'd done.

"I don't," Eric said, lowering his voice.

"Exactly. You don't know. I've heard from the others. Dead ends. All of them. You were our only bet on capturing the ritual."

"We recorded the beginning," Eric said firmly, a drop of sweat rolling down the side of his face.

"That's better than nothing, but your defiance will set us back. We had an opportunity to review the ritual from start to finish, and you squandered it."

The weight on Leah lifted for just a moment.

"It wasn't his fault!" Leah shouted. She clenched her fists, holding back the tremor that she felt in her hands.

"Silence, Pawn," Constance said, glaring at her.

Leah wavered in her stance and shook her head. "It was me. I couldn't simply stand by and watch without doing something. It was me. I killed . . ."

Constance shifted and stepped in front of Leah. "I don't need *Tiferet* to know what happened, Pawn. Your Black Knight can't seem to rein you in."

Eric cleared his throat. "White Bishop Berkenshire, please, I—"

Constance raised her hand, and Eric silenced immediately. "No more from you. Failing to control your Pawn is a poor reflection on all of us."

Leah reached for Constance's arm. "It wasn't him! He did what he could to stop me. This was my fault. I couldn't just stand there and let it happen. Not again. Please. If you punish anyone, punish me, and *only* me."

"Enough," Constance said. "Your actions directly

violated the Infinity Board's orders. You're lucky I haven't stripped you of all rights and tossed you in the cell with that thing already." Constance paused, waiting with her eye on Leah. Once enough time passed, she nodded. "But it would seem you still have some restraint when you want it. Cellar duty, tonight. I don't care if you're tired. Since you brought that creature into this academy, you can watch over it and make sure it doesn't escape. After that, we can discuss your future with the Queen's Gambit and the Infinity Board."

Sid escorted Leah down the stairwell to the back of the kitchen. She could feel disappointment lingering in her *Yesod* bond as Eric remained with Constance.

Fluorescent bulbs flickered to life above her, flooding half the space in a cold, dull light. The light wasn't enough to reach the last cellar, the one containing a mass lying in the center.

Sid pulled out a small stool and handed her a gun and a radio. "If anything goes bad, shoot first. I don't want you or anyone else in any more danger." He turned and started for the stairs. Before he reached them, he paused. "I would do everything in your power to stay awake. If anyone catches you sleeping on the job, you're likely to end up in one of these instead."

"Thanks for the advice," she said, taking a seat on the stool as Sid headed back up the stairs.

As her eyes adjusted, she peered at the chimera lying in the center of the last cell. When he woke, he'd see the small cell they put him in, with a thin mattress topper on a concrete slab and a tiny metal toilet. Better than almost dying, Leah supposed. Still, her stomach turned in knots just thinking about how this man had been treated before he even woke.

Time didn't seem to matter in the cellar. With the fluorescent fixtures as the only source of light inside this windowless, concrete-walled prison, Leah had no sense of what the outside world was doing. Hours felt like they passed by as her eyes grew heavy. She wasn't sure if she fell asleep or was lost in a malaise of boredom, but when she nearly fell off her chair, she jumped to her feet, pacing the five feet she had, back and forth, underneath the light.

She still couldn't get the woman's face out of her head. Couldn't stop seeing the tears in her eyes. She knew the Infinity Board would only see that she had made a mistake, and she suspected they'd eventually move past it. But could she? Did she even want to?

A sound came from above, followed by a creaking from the stairs. Leah froze, her hand instinctively wrapping around her gun.

The light shone on Gabe, descending onto the last step, carrying a small white bowl. He stifled a yawn and grinned. "Morning. Trying to make the rest of us look bad by taking on extra duties?"

"Morning? What time is it?" Leah asked, relaxing her grip on the gun.

He handed her the bowl, filled with warm oatmeal topped with a sprinkling of cinnamon and fresh blueber-ries, and a folded napkin with the distinct smell of bacon. "Four. I saw Sid bring you down here late last night. Couldn't get it out of my head, so I got up early. I knew you were safe, but I didn't know what they had you doing."

Leah's stomach growled as she dipped her spoon into the oatmeal. The nutty flavors of the slightly toasted oats and brown sugar exploded her taste buds. "They seriously need to let you cook more. This is so good."

Gabe shrugged. "It's nothing. I needed an excuse to get out of bed this early."

"Well, thanks," Leah said, a smile spreading across her face.

Leah unwrapped the napkin and found three strips of crispy bacon inside. He'd cooked them perfectly, and it looked exactly like the bacon she'd once mistakenly had when she was younger and didn't know better.

She cleared her throat and handed back the wrapped napkin. Her cheeks warmed, and she said, "Thanks, but I can't. I'm kosher."

"Oh, uh. I'm sorry," Gabe said, his cheeks turning red.

"It's fine, you didn't know." Leah extended the bacon to him. "You want it?"

Gabe smiled and took it. "Thanks." He picked at the bacon. "Did they tell you what they're going to do with the chimera?"

Leah shook her head. "They just tossed me down here and went on their way. They acted like they didn't even want him here, but I bet the minute he wakes, they'll start interrogating him. Otherwise, why not kill him? They think they're going to get information out of him."

"With no thanks to you, I bet." His eyes met hers and flitted away.

Leah dropped her gaze to the ground. "Yeah." She paused, her fingertips went numb, and her hand shook. "I . . . I killed someone."

He stepped close and clasped his hand on hers, steading the shake. "Saving him?" He gestured to the chimera.

Leah nodded.

"Against the Infinity Board's orders," he said.

"What's that supposed to mean?" Leah asked, looking him in the eyes.

"Nothing. Just that you had the courage to do something right, and you saved someone. You stepped up, but you're beating yourself up. I wish I had that courage."

Leah smirked. "I suppose that's my mom's hardheaded blood in me. Guess it pays off to have stubborn parents."

Gabe looked away at that. "I wish my mom wasn't as stubborn."

Leah nearly dropped the bowl. "No, I didn't mean . . . I—"

"It's okay. I'm pretty sure I didn't tell you the entire story."

Leah caught his gaze and shrugged. "Unless he wakes up, I have nothing else to do but listen."

Gabe paused for a long moment. Then, when Leah was about to wave it off, he started. "They were both part of the Infinity Board. Knights. I practically grew up with a knife in one hand and a gun in the other. They disciplined me better than any army or military could. Yet, the one time I stepped out of line, the one time my little childish brain thought it was okay to disobey, my dad died."

Leah took in a sharp breath as her heart ached in her chest. She set the bowl down on the stool and hugged him without a second thought. "I'm sorry."

He reciprocated, his warm arms and sweet oak scent wrapping around her. "I was six. If I'd known then that I was too young, that it wasn't my fault, maybe I'd see things differently. My nan fought with my mother for years. She advocated for me. Pointed out all the dangers that they brought home with them. My mom didn't care, just shipped me off to be with my nan, and that was that. At least there, I finally got to hone my cooking skills and learn to use a knife to heal rather than kill."

Leah pulled back slightly, just enough to see Gabe face to face. "Why didn't you stay with her?"

He pulled away, shaking his head. "Obedience, I guess. When the call came, what else was I supposed to do? Either way, I'm here now. Exactly where my parents planned for me to be since I was born."

"You were a kid. That wasn't fair."

Gabriel backed up against the wall and chuckled, wiping his face. "Just an obedient kid. Still am. Was. That is . . . until you started talking to me."

"Me? Why?"

"Sure, you're stubborn like you said. But I'd call it strong-willed. They tried to break you, and you didn't even flinch."

Leah blinked, processing what he said. If only he knew how much she'd questioned herself along the way.

Gabe pushed off the wall. "I just mean that you're like a little beacon of hope. Even through all this, you're still *you*." He rubbed the back of his neck and shook his head. "That's sounds stupid. I just meant—"

He didn't have a chance to finish his words. Leah walked forward, her heart pounding in her chest as she grabbed his face and planted a kiss on his lips, feeling the stubble on his chin. She took a step back, biting her lip. "Sorry. I—I know you and Joanna are . . ."

Gabe's eyes widened, and he shook his head. "She broke it off. Seems like I wasn't doing enough to keep her attention."

Relief spread over Leah, and she let out a massive sigh. "Well then, I guess you know where I stand."

Gabe stepped forward and kissed her back, his soft lips pressed against hers, and his hand caressed her cheek. He moved back and smiled. "And now you know where I stand."

Leah cleared her throat and looked back at the chimera, still lying in the shadows. "You should get back upstairs before anyone else sees you interfering with guard duty. Thanks for the uh . . . oatmeal."

Gabe took the bowl and smiled. "Any time. And I'll hold the bacon next time."

He planted another kiss on her cheek and turned, racing up the steps before she could say another word.

CHAPTER 12

A PECULIAR PRISONER

Leah thought about the kiss as she sat back down on the stool. She could taste the hint of bacon on his lips, and it sent a wave of guilt through her. He was Joanna's boyfriend. Leah's friend. She couldn't honestly think this was a good idea. The guilt tried to pull at her happiness, but she forced it down, focusing on Gabe and the smile on his face.

More time passed in the cellars, and the stool Leah sat on shifted and changed underneath her. Armrests formed, and a backing supported her as she opened her eyes. The large marble table formed, and Asmodeus sat in a similar chair across from her.

He looked just as thin as last time, with bags underneath his black eyes. "Hello, little lovebird."

Leah frowned at him. "That has nothing to do with you."

Asmodeus stretched in his chair, craning his long neck from side to side and twisting his back. "Why do you keep doing this to us?"

Leah blinked a couple times, realizing how sore she was and how the stretches he did seemed to be the ones she wanted to do. "Us? There is no us. You wanted me to kill those people. I killed someone, and you said nothing. I was . . . alone."

Asmodeus rapped his long fingers on the table and looked off into the distance. "We are in this together. Your actions and mine are the reason we are still here. Do you really think that demon was going to let that poor woman go back to seeing her child?"

Leah pushed against the table, but her chair didn't slide back. She was stuck. Imprisoned across from him. "Did you bring me here to lecture me some more? Make me feel like killing her was some mercy? Did you see her eyes?"

His eyes locked on hers as he pushed away from the table and stood. He strained and winced but never lost his eye contact. "My kind in this world are . . . what's the best word to use . . . ah . . . parasites? We feed and feed, giving back what we can to our people before the host dies. That woman would have been a puppet to that demon until the day she no longer breathed."

Leah grabbed her left arm and squeezed hard, digging her nails into her flesh. "If you're a parasite, then what's stopping me from pulling you out?"

"We share a common enemy. The more we fight, and the more you resist, the more energy you waste. Our best chance of facing off with Legion is together."

Leah scoffed and pulled her hand off her arm, eyeing the little half-moon cuts she'd made. "So what? I just let you take over? No way. You already made me use the Tree of Death. Who's saying you aren't turning me into the next William or Jade?"

Asmodeus pursed his lips and placed his hands behind his back. He turned and looked out into the dark abyss that surrounded them. "Legion can end everything. Demons and humans. He is an endless pit of hunger. The Valley is in worse shape from his reign, and the scraps of energy barely held my fellow demons who were outside his reach together. Your world is ripe for the taking. At least, in Legion's eyes, and he won't stop until everything you see is his. Do you want that? Your friends? Eric? All taken and drained to feed Legion?"

Images flashed through her mind. Her friends possessed by demons. Eric chained up and suffocating for an eternity. Calling out, screaming her name. "Of course not."

"I marked you so I could stay and fight Legion. To right my wrongs and stand up against that . . . *thing*. I was once Kyjak, a ruler, but he took everything from me, even my will. Mystics can't defeat him alone."

Leah placed her elbows on the table, holding her head in her hands. He was right, and she knew it. She could feel it, as clear as the *Yesod* bond she had with Eric.

Asmodeus turned back to the table and rested his pale hands on the back of his chair. "I know this isn't easy for you. But for now, just lower your resistance. Let me in, just a little. If we do this together, then there's no stopping us. We'll get stronger, together, and we might stand a chance against Legion."

Leah stared into his black eyes, into the void of darkness that held a tiny white point of light in each. "I . . ."

The shake of a metal door tore Leah from her dream, nearly toppling off the stool.

Her arm ached, and jolts of pain shot up and down her arm. She pulled up her shirt sleeve to see the tiny cuts she'd given herself in her dream marking her skin as if they had been there for days.

Metal struck again, and she followed the sound to the cell shrouded in shadows. Her eyes warmed as *Tiferet* triggered, and the room flooded in light.

She saw it then, the chimera, testing the door to his cellar. She pushed herself off the stool and walked closer to his cell, his musky scent growing stronger as she closed in.

"Um, hi."

The chimera bleated and backed away. In the dark, Leah could see the dull green shine of the chimera's eyes as he stared at her.

"I'm Leah Ackerman. What's your name?"

When he spoke, his voice wavered, sounding like a mix between a human and a goat. "Where? Where am I?"

"You're safe," she looked at his cell and frowned, "for now."

He stepped forward. Leah traced her eyes along the horns protruding from his head and curving to either side like a ram. He sniffed the air. "I . . . I . . . recognize your scent. You . . . saved me."

Leah looked down. "I did."

He turned his head left, then right, giving both his rectangular pupils time to stare directly at her and the steps leading out of the cellar. "But they didn't take that well, I assume? You're tired, yet down here with me."

Leah nodded. "My orders were to observe and not intervene. I didn't exactly listen."

The chimera's ears twitched, and he tilted his head, still swaying as he spoke. "I see." He paused and cocked his head. "Why me?"

Warmth spread in Leah's cheeks, and she bit her lip. "You're the first chimera we've seen alive since Paige was with us. I wanted . . . I needed—Do you know if she is still out there? If she's safe?"

The chimera took his time responding, slowly walking closer to the bars. "I recall a sister who once went by that name, Paige. I only saw her once before she joined the other night hunters."

"Night hunters?"

The chimera's ears twitched, and he turned his head back and forth, his eyes fighting to keep a focus on her. "Others like her. Predators of the night and protectors of the weak."

"Sounds like her. Was she a wolf? That's what that doctor forced her to become."

The man shook his head. "No one forces a human to turn."

Leah frowned. "Dr. Toppen did. That monster kidnapped us at the academy."

"Dr. Toppen is a pioneer, restoring our kind back to our glory. She's not a monster. She's a saint. My kin are finally returning, after centuries of hunting since the fall of Rome."

"But they forced Paige. And Dr. Toppen was working with a demon. How can you say she's a saint? Are you honestly going to sit here and tell me you're happy with what she's doing?"

The creature's eyes drooped. "Rigel."

"What?"

"You asked for my name. It's Rigel. If you are going to continue berating my way of life, you should at least know my name."

Leah took a step back from the cell. "I'm sorry. It's just that Dr. Toppen was going to turn me against my will."

"The agreement Dr. Toppen made was her only means of finding our kin among the Mystics. Abducting them was part of their plan, but we offered those that wanted it an alternative. No one can force a human to turn. We embrace it as a first step toward becoming whole."

Leah shook her head. "No. Paige wouldn't have. She—"

"She was unhappy, no? Wrapped too deeply in the turmoil of expectation and wanted to make a life of her own choosing. Same as me. Same as all of us. She was given a choice and found her true calling."

"But Dr. Toppen kidnapped others. Joanna. Me."

Rigel turned away. "Part of the agreement. Nasty business working with those demons. But our survival depended on it."

"And what about you? Were you ready to willingly sacrifice yourself when they strung you up to that tree?"

"No." He paced his cell, eyeing Leah. "She shouldn't have made that first deal. Now we are paying the price. Their last demand was unforgivable. Something the likes of shifters would do, not us."

"What demand? Who did she make that deal with? Legion?"

Rigel approached the cell bars, his face pressed up against the bars and tears forming in his goat-like eyes. "I don't know. They wouldn't let Dr. Toppen go. She had to agree to their new terms. It wasn't her fault."

"What wasn't her fault?"

"The children."

Leah felt her stomach turn. "What children? Are you saying that Dr. Toppen is turning—"

"No. She couldn't. It isn't our way. She refused. We all refused. They took us for it. Hunted us down. But they still have them. The children. And I don't know what they plan to do with them next."

"Where?"

CHAPTER 13
THE BIGGER PICTURE

The cellar door slammed open, and two Black Knights with guns and tactical gear headed down the stairs.

"Ackerman. White Bishop Berkenshire requests your presence." The Knight speaking was Alan Kowen. Leah had seen him around a few times before but never spoke with him. His scar, a mark that trailed down the left side of his face from the short-cropped black hair on his head down to his clean-shaven chin, shone in the overhead light.

"Wait, no. I almost . . ." She looked back at the chimera, who'd settled into the corner of his cage, eyes shut as if he had been asleep this entire time.

Alan wrapped his hand around her arm and pulled.

"Let go of me!" Leah shouted, pulling against the guard.

"Orders were clear. Come now, and let's do this the easy way."

Leah tugged against the grip but complied, following them up the stairs. Her mind reeled over the information Rigel had supplied, from discovering that humans willingly turn into chimeras to their involvement with demons. And through it all, she believed him.

They reached the doors, and the Knight holding her arm cleared his throat.

"Come in," White Bishop Berkenshire called from the office.

Morning light streaming in from the windows of the office blinded Leah as the smell coffee filled her nostrils. When her vision adjusted, she found the French press resting haphazardly on Constance's disorganized desk. The White Bishop rose from her seat, the map behind her now with even more red and black pins covering it. She gestured toward the press. "Care for some?"

Leah nodded, and Constance pulled two mugs from a drawer, wiping them out with her hand. She poured coffee into each cup and handed one to Leah. "You'll have to drink it black," Constance said before looking at the Knights still standing in the room. "That will be all for now. She can see her way back. Thank you, Knight Kowen."

Alan clicked his heels together. "Yes, White Bishop Berkenshire." He turned and left, closing the door behind him.

"Please, sit," Constance said, gesturing at the chair in front of her.

Cupping the mug in her hands, Leah did as she was requested and sat down.

Constance grabbed a stack of papers on her desk and plopped them on the floor. She pulled off her glasses and took a long drink from her mug before locking eyes with Leah. "I hope cellar duty has been treating you well."

Leah took a sip from her mug. Over steeped, cold coffee filled her mouth, and she forced it down. "Yes, but Rigel, he—"

"Yes, *White Bishop*," Constance corrected her.

Leah choked back both a sigh and the desire to roll her

eyes. "Yes, White Bishop Berkenshire. Rigel believes that there are children—"

Constance held up her hand. "We know. Once you got that thing to start talking, I told Nykima to intercept with her Knights. Any information that thing gives will need to be confirmed and vetted."

Leah's face paled. They had been listening in. Did they hear her and Gabe? Of course they had. "But Rigel was about to tell me! He would have, had the Knights not barged in."

"They barged in because you got him talking. Our inter-rogators will do the rest. We can't have him spouting half-truths in your head. Or did you seem to forget what their doctor was doing to your friends?"

Leah's heart pounded loudly in her head. They'd used her and tossed her aside when they didn't need her. She clenched her fist and bit her lip. "Yes, White Bishop Berkenshire."

She nodded. "Seems like cellar duty suited you well. Hopefully you're starting to understand your place in the Infinity Board. You are dismissed, Pawn."

Leah pushed her chair back and stood. Knots formed in her stomach, and the words blurted out before she could stop them. "White Bishop, may I ask a question?"

Constance stifled a yawn and eyed Leah's mug of barely drunk coffee. "You going to finish that?"

Leah frowned. "No. Do you—?"

Before she could finish her sentence, Constance reached across the desk, grabbed the coffee, and finished it in one gulp. "Go ahead. What do you want to ask?"

"What will they do with him?"

Constance took her glasses off, rubbed her eyes, and said, "When the guards get their hands on it, they will interrogate it at the behest of the council. If it chooses not to cooperate, then the Rooks will send an order to imprison it."

A pit dropped in Leah's stomach. "No, you can't. He was about to tell me everything."

Constance rose from her seat and rested her fingertips on the table. "Then if *he* was so willing to confide in you, there shouldn't be an issue with a proper interrogation where we can vet his information."

Leah chewed on her lower lip and took in a deep breath, steadying herself before she spoke. "With all due respect, White Bishop, I don't understand why you cut me off from talking to him. Even if he lied, it would have been something to go off of. Now, instead, you are putting him in a room with people he doesn't trust—"

"We found something at the ritual site," Constance said, cutting Leah off.

Leah stared; her eyebrow raised.

"I had Nykima stop by the site before the cleanup crew showed up. The demons you took care of. One of them had a badge to an orphanage. When that thing indicated it knew about the children, we had to intervene. We suspect anything to do with children, which I truly hope there is nothing, would be easily hidden in the confines of an orphanage."

"But they're kids," Leah said. "I thought demons left them alone because their energy was unstable."

Constance nodded. "They are too chaotic for demons to handle. If they have an interest now, then I worry about what that could imply. Either way, I'm running out of patience."

Leah frowned while Constance looked past her to the door, then she cleared her throat. "Well, best for you to be off. You're dismissed, Pawn. Tell the Knights outside to bring Sid and Grace to me, please."

"Please, don't hurt him."

Constance gave a slight nod and settled back down into her chair, her fingers rubbing at her temples. "We will do what's necessary, but I'll order them to consult with me before leaping to drastic measures."

CHAPTER 14

HARD TRUTHS

"The cellar girl lives!" Sarah shouted as Leah stepped into the third-floor common room.

"The cellar girl needs a nap," Leah said, stifling a yawn and glaring at the morning light gleaming into the room.

Isaac's head popped up from a red couch next to Sarah. "Finally, we can get some answers."

Sarah nodded. "If Ricardo opens his damn mouth again with what he thinks he heard, I'm gonna knock him out."

"What are they saying?" Leah collapsed onto the couch next to Sarah.

"He claims he heard Eric talking to Grace. Says you went rogue, killed a bunch of demons, and there's a chimera in the basement. Of course, they won't tell us anything, and Miranda started claiming you were dead. Gabe squashed that pretty quick last night. Said he saw you get taken to the cellars, but that was it."

Leah's head lifted at the sound of Gabe's name and looked around the common room.

Isaac hopped up on the edge of his seat. "They're all in the library. I hooked up the monitor and broke through the firewall. Then someone got annoyed with her girlfriend's attitude."

Sarah shot Isaac a glare. "Miranda is *not* my girlfriend. She's apparently not into girls, thank you very much. And I was more annoyed with Ricardo than her egging him on."

Leah took in a sharp breath and blurted out the words before she could think to stop herself. "I don't know how much Constance and the others want this under wraps, but . . . I didn't kill them. Not all of them. I . . . I killed one. But I couldn't let that chimera die knowing I could have helped. Eric couldn't stop me, I just did it." Tears streamed down her face as the images flashed in her mind. "She said she had a kid. I killed her. Her kid doesn't have a mom anymore. They're . . ."

Sarah wrapped an arm around her and shook her head. "Stop. They were possessed. What else could you have done?"

Isaac nodded. "You did what you had to."

Sarah gripped Leah's shoulder and squeezed. "Dude, you saved a chimera and took out demons. Badass demon hunter over here."

"Badass indeed," Isaac agreed.

Leah scoffed. "But Constance tossed him in the cellars. Then, when he started talking to me, the guards came for me and took me to Constance's office. But . . . she said something odd."

Sarah leaned in closer. "What?"

"She said she was running out of patience. Like she's fed up with the informants or something. Maybe it was nothing."

Isaac shrugged. "Or she thinks someone higher up is feeding her misinformation. It isn't like members can't be corrupted, right? I mean, remember the dean? It isn't like the past months haven't been dead end after dead end."

Leah looked down at her hands. "Maybe. I'm still sick of how she used me to get the chimera to talk. It all feels wrong."

"Who knows?" Sarah said. "I mean, if you were down there watching him, and not a guard, maybe it was her way of keeping this within the Queen's Gambit. Maybe someone like Sid is questioning him instead of the guards. They all report to someone else. She could be keeping them in the dark."

Isaac nodded. "I'd do that. Wait for the right moment and move in quick before security can get confirmation from headquarters."

They sat for a moment, Leah staring down at her hands while Isaac and Sarah stared off in opposite directions.

Leah broke the silence, clearing her throat. "So, bottom line. We still can't really trust anyone."

"I'd say we can't trust security for sure," Isaac said. "But between the three of us, we're practically bonded to everyone in the Gambit one way or another. That should count for something."

"I don't know," Sarah said. "There're still some I wouldn't trust as far as I could throw them. Like Brandon."

That name sparked something inside Leah, and she took in a sharp breath. "There was something else. Rigel, the chimera, said no one can force someone to turn into a chimera; it's a choice. So, Paige and Theodore, they chose to be chimeras. He said there was no other way."

"Well, that sounds like bullshit," Isaac said.

Leah nodded. "I thought so at first, but I'm inclined to believe him. He was telling the truth, but I don't know how to explain how I know. I just do."

"So, what does that mean? Do we give up on Paige, then?" Sarah asked.

Leah waited a moment, weighing her answer. "No. I

might believe him, but I still want to hear it from her. I'm not willing to give up on Paige until I know she wants this."

Isaac ran his fingers through his hair. "We could also talk to Brandon."

Both Leah and Sarah frowned.

He cleared his throat and continued. "Well, if you choose to be a chimera, then maybe Brandon would know if Theodore would have wanted it. He'd know if his brother was unhappy, right?"

Leah's stomach churned at the thought of Theodore. Her friends still didn't know what she'd done.

Sarah let out a sarcastic laugh. "Yeah, why don't we talk to Brandon? Are you crazy? Even a hint of his brother's name sets him off."

Leah pushed herself up off the couch. "But Isaac has a point. That would be our quickest way of knowing Rigel wasn't lying. We just need to bring it up at the right time."

Sarah rolled her eyes. "And when would that be?"

Leah stifled a yawn. "The sooner the better."

"Why don't you catch a few hours of sleep?" Isaac suggested, standing and starting toward the doors. "We'll get you later and we can do it then?"

Leah nodded and looked at her bed. At least she'd get some rest before being tossed into more chaos. She relaxed, thinking about being wrapped up in blankets. Safe and warm.

Sarah stood, heading over to join Isaac when Leah said, "Wait, Sarah, can you stay a second?"

Isaac paused at the doors, "Keeping secrets from me?"

"It's girl stuff," Leah said.

Sarah sighed and looked over her shoulder at Isaac, "Go now, save yourself."

"You don't have to tell me twice," Isaac said, vanishing beyond the doors.

Sarah found a spot back on the couches, looking up at the ceiling. "So, spill the beans."

"Well, I don't know if I should. But I have to tell someone. I think. I don't know."

"Leah, what is it?"

Leah breathed in a shaky breath. "Gabe and I kissed."

Sarah nearly fell off the couch as she righted herself. "Wait! What? How? When?"

Leah sat next to Sarah and looked up at the ceiling. "He snuck into the cellar. It sort of just happened."

"What about Joanna?"

"They broke up." Leah said. "At least, that's what he told me."

Sarah punched Leah's shoulder and laughed. "You're screwed if she finds out. Homewrecker!"

"I know. I know. It was dumb. But . . ."

"But?"

"But I don't regret it happening ," Lead admitted.

"What now?" Sarah asked.

Leah shrugged. "I don't know. Nothing?"

Sarah laughed. "So he was a bad kisser?"

Leah felt heat rise into her cheeks. "No! I didn't say that! It was good. Look, I just needed to tell someone. I did, and now I'm going to bed," she said, standing up.

As Leah walked to her dorm room, Sarah chased after her. "Leah Ackerman! You can't drop that bombshell and go to bed! You better tell me everything this instant, or I'll beat it out of you."

Leah groaned and plopped down on her bed. "It all happened so fast."

Sarah sat down by Leah's feet.

"Well, who kissed first?" Sarah asked.

"I did."

"And did he kiss you back?"

"Yes. His stubble tickled my chin." Leah let out a single laugh, then sighed.

Sarah frowned. "But?"

"Well, there was one thing." Leah took a deep breath. "I don't think my mom or dad would approve."

Sarah frowned. "Why? Gabe's like the nicest guy I know."

Leah picked at her fingers. "It's not that. He's not . . ." Leah felt a lump forming in her throat. "He's not Jewish."

"Why does that matter?" Sarah asked.

"I don't know. Both my parents always wanted me to be with a nice Jewish boy."

"Can't he convert or something?" Sarah shrugged. "He might. You never know."

Leah shook her head. "Converting is not that simple."

Sarah leaned over and punched Leah's shoulder. "Come on. You're sixteen. It's not like you're going to marry him."

Leah buried her face in her hands, her cheeks growing hot. "I know. It's stupid, I know. But I can't ask my parents. Instead, I just have this guilt in the pit of my stomach." Her voice cracked, and she leaned forward, resting her elbows on her knees. "I just always pictured it would be like the two of them. Like something I have to do. Something bigger than me."

"I get it," Sarah said. "But you should have a little fun now and then, right? I'm not going to let you run off and marry the guy at sixteen, okay? Give it a few months, at least, until we're out of this damn academy and making a name for ourselves."

Leah lifted her head and smiled. "Maybe? I don't know."

CHAPTER 15

SKELETONS IN THE CLOSET

The next day, the trio stepped into the library and heard Miranda's voice carry from the corner of the room. "I don't know what to tell you. I don't get it either."

As they passed by the shelves of books and found the nook, they spotted Ricardo and Joanna sprawled out on the couches and Miranda resting against the windowsill.

Leah said, "Have any of you see Bran—"

Her eyes met Gabe's, and something fluttered in her chest. The kiss from last night replayed in her mind.

"Finally," Joanna said, cutting off her daydream. "There she is. Now you two can stop bickering and just ask her what happened."

Ricardo sat up immediately and glared at Leah. "Did you do it? Sabotage your duty and save a chimera?"

Gabe rolled his eyes. "I already told you."

Sarah stepped forward, her fists clenched. Leah grabbed her wrist and pulled, preventing her from moving any closer to Ricardo. "She saved someone from being sacrificed, you dick," Sarah said.

Miranda stood up, her eyes wide. "So, you did it? Defied a direct order? One of those things is here?"

Joanna scoffed. "Of course she did. She's not a goodie-two-shoes like you, Mira. And she's too special not to get kicked out, or did you forget that too? Pretty sure she could burn the whole academy down and no one would bat an—"

"Shut up, Jo." Gabe said.

Joanna turned and huffed. "What did you say?"

"He said shut up," Isaac said.

"I'm not special," Leah said. "I paid for defying orders."

Ricardo shook his head, and his cheeks flared red. "You really think that? You're still here. If I put a toe out of line, they'd cut me out of the Gambit in a heartbeat. You saved our enemy, and if the rumor is right, you killed someone doing it. So don't give me this moral high ground bullshit."

Sarah yanked on Leah's grip and pulled free, standing face to face with Ricardo. "You have a problem with it, you have a problem with me."

Joanna let out a laugh. "And there's the bodyguard, making sure no one says anything wrong about poor little Leah."

"Cut it, Jo," Miranda said.

"What's your problem?" Gabe asked.

Joanna hopped up off the couch and shrugged. "Just making an observation." She looked at Gabe and raised an eyebrow. "Well, this has been fun, but I've got somewhere else to be."

"Where are you—" Gabe started, but she slipped between Sarah and Ricardo, vanishing between the shelves before he could finish.

Leah gave him a half smile.

Ricardo backed up and slumped on the couch. "I just

mean that I was stuck running perimeter checks for a week for stating an opinion to a White Bishop. It seems unfair compared to how many times Leah's cut off, or outright defied, orders."

Leah nodded. "You're right. I don't know why I've gotten away with so much. But, had Rigel not started speaking, I'd probably still be down there watching him."

"Leah are you in here?" came a voice shouting through the library.

The voice was Brandon's, and the cold sweat formed on Leah's brow. "Yeah," she called back.

He rounded the stacks and met her gaze. "Grace asked me to come get you. She's waiting outside."

Leah turned back to Isaac and whispered, "Remember Constance's orders. No one else can know."

Isaac nodded before turning to the others. "Hey, who wants to help me torrent some movies?"

Brandon and Leah walked in silence. Her heart pounded in her chest until she finally spit it out. "We need to talk."

He stopped and looked her in the eyes, the same brown eyes that his brother Theodore had. "What's up?"

"You heard about the chimera in the basement, right?"

His face immediately changed, his eyebrows frowning and hatred filling his eyes. "I did."

Leah took in a deep breath, her voice cracking as she spoke. "I was on cellar duty last night. He spoke to me. Told me about his kind."

Brandon reached out, grabbing Leah's shoulder. "Did it tell you why they took my brother from me?"

She looked away. "According to the chimera, they can't force anyone to change. Theodore and Paige, the chimera said the change only happens if they wanted it to."

Brandon squeezed hard on her shoulder, and Leah winced before he let go. "Of course it would tell you that. But you *know* the chimeras abducted them. They took Theo from his bed in the middle of the night."

Leah nodded. "They did, but it was part of the deal with the Dean. If Theo wasn't taken by the chimeras, then he would have ended up possessed. I know it's hard to believe, but it was the way he said it, and what I saw in Paige's eyes. I just wonder if maybe—"

Brandon took a step back. "You're telling me my brother willingly left me to become this . . . thing? Why?"

"I don't know. He said it was an opportunity to control their own lives. Start new."

All the anger bled out from Brandon, and his shoulders slumped. "He . . . left me? But why? That doesn't make sense. Theo wouldn't do that."

Nykima's warning echoed in Leah's mind. "I'm sorry. Don't do anything brash. Please. I just thought you, of all people, should know."

He nodded, his eyes trained on the ground. "I've been trying not to think about it. Hoping it wasn't true. But it makes sense. And it hurts. We went through everything together. When our mom was finally smart enough to leave Dad. Him finding us years later. He protected me, you know. Took the scissors off the counter, he was barely seven, and stabbed him. Didn't know it was already too late. Mom was dead. Dad now too. It was supposed to be the two of us, through thick and thin."

Leah grabbed his hand. "I . . . I didn't know."

He took a step back, his eyes listless as he pulled his

hand. "Grace is waiting. Field two. You know how to get there."

"Brandon . . ."

He turned away from her, heading up the stairs and out of sight.

CHAPTER 16
BISHOP'S WISDOM

Leah stepped outside and found Grace sitting in the practice field, the sun shining down on her dark skin and brown hair. The woman sat perfectly still, her arms resting on her knees and her eyes closed.

The air gelled and thickened as Leah moved closer. A cool breeze blew past her and toward Grace, swirling around and tossing her hair left and right. Goosebumps prickled across her arms, and Leah's chest grew tight.

Each step made Leah's jaw ache a little more, the energy emanating off Grace almost too strong to handle. Then the White Bishop opened her eyes and the sensation vanished.

"Glad to see you, Pawn Ackerman."

Leah put her heels together and placed her hands behind her back. "You summoned me, White Bishop?"

Standing, Grace brushed off her dark red leggings and white crop top, the silver bangles around her wrists jingling as she did so. "At ease. Join me for my walk."

Grace didn't wait for Leah to accept. She turned and started toward the woods, past the fields. Leah raced to keep up with Grace's brisk pace, the warm breeze pushing them along.

Neither spoke as they entered the woods through a dirt path until they came upon a river at the border of the forest. Leah traced the path up the river, remembering the twists and turns that led up to the destroyed dock only a few hundred feet away.

"You've been quite the rebel, Leah."

She stopped and glared at Grace's back. So, this was Constance's plan. Use Grace to make Leah fall in line. She dug her nails into her palm. "He was going to die if I did nothing. If it makes me a rebel to save someone instead of following orders, then yeah, I am. Not like the Board, which hasn't given us anything but dead ends and false hope."

Grace knelt by the riverbed and picked up a stone. "Save one life, take another. And this isn't the first casualty you've left in your wake."

Leah looked back down the path they had come, wondering what Grace might do if she turned and left now. Instead, she stood her ground. "With all due respect, White Bishop, I've already had this conversation with White Bishop Berkenshire."

Grace skipped the stone across the river, managing three before it sank beneath the surface. "I know. But you haven't had the conversation with *me*."

"Okay," Leah said. "I'm listening."

Grace picked up another stone and turned to Leah. "Constance is awaiting orders from the Board for a recon mission to validate what information the chimera has given us."

Leah stepped forward. "Then you see it, don't you? Rigel told us about the children. We know where they might be. Why are we waiting on orders if we can just see for ourselves? Think of how many people we might lose if we keep waiting."

"So, you prefer we go in blind, without ensuring that the Infinity Board has allocated resources and backup if we end up face to face with Legion?"

Leah paused. She hadn't thought about that, hadn't considered what would happen if they ran into Legion and didn't have enough people to take him down. She looked past Grace, out at the river, and didn't say another word.

Grace held out her hand and placed the stone in Leah's palm. "When I was your age, I had that same need to get things done, that same hard-headed faith that I knew best. I don't blame you. People like us, people who experience trauma and awaken this power inside, we can't sit still and let someone else call the shots. Our need for revenge fuels every waking second."

Leah shook her head, feeling the cold sweat rise on the back of her neck. "But we can't act on revenge. Eric told me that. Else we'd give in to the tree of death. I don't know what you're trying to get me to say, but revenge doesn't fuel me. It can't fuel me."

"Maybe not, but you can't deny that you hold that anger somewhere. Why else would you be so apt to speak out to your superiors? Or when you take initiative in defiance of a direct order. You might think you have control, but have you considered where that energy goes if you bottle it up?"

Leah looked out to the river and tossed her stone. It splashed and sank beneath the surface without a single skip. She then walked toward the riverbed and plucked up another one and tossed it in her hands.

Grace walked up beside her, peering out to the river. "You've been through more than most Mystics, most Knights even. Facing down the demon that caused this energy to wake inside you and cast him back from where he came."

Leah looked up at Grace's brown eyes. *Could she know?* A twinge surged up her arm, Asmodeus sending the same concern.

Leah half-heartedly tossed the stone, managing a single skip. "And now he can't come after me."

Grace nodded. "You faced your greatest enemy and took him down. But now what? Have you even given yourself the time you need to mourn? No. Instead, you faced off against chimeras, corrupted Mystics, and now against Legion. The life of a Mystic is demanding, but if you bury your head in this line of work, you will always find an evil to extinguish."

"What else should I do? Just let that evil win?"

Grace shook her head. "I brought you out here so we could speak in private, away from listening ears. You weren't summoned so I could scold you. I just needed you to know that you aren't alone. So, this burden you carry, you don't have to carry it by yourself. You have two wonderful friends, and a class of Pawns all waiting for someone amongst them to show them what it means to be a Mystic. Don't let the bureaucracy of the Infinity Board discourage you."

Leah tilted her head. "Wait, so you agree that something is wrong? Why don't you ever speak up, then?"

Grace picked up another stone and juggled it in her hands. "Like you, I was once a White Pawn angry at the world. A young White Bishop came to me and taught me something I have told no one else." She tossed the stone and turned without another word, following the path up the river.

Leah eyed the boathouse as they passed it. Memories surfaced of the last time she was there, facing off against chimeras and William. No one had come back to fix the massive hole in the wall, or the burns.

Grace walked few paces ahead of her now, stepping through a copse of trees. Leah raced to follow and came upon a clearing. Inside was a garden filled with various breeds of flowers.

Turning around in the center of the clearing, Grace held her hands together. "The Infinity Board is simply a group of people, no different from you and me. The only thing that holds us all together is the common goal to maintain balance and protect humanity at all costs."

Leah ran her fingers along the blue irises next to her. "But if we all have the same goal, then why does it take so long to get anything done?"

Grace smiled. "And there is the other side of it, the part no one will admit out loud, but the reason for the bureaucracy. We protect the world from other Mystics too."

Leah paused for a second, letting this sink in. "So, what then? We let people die just waiting around for the Infinity Board to weigh in?"

"Do you think William was a fluke?"

Leah looked at Grace for a moment and shook her head.

Grace sighed and traced her eyes around the garden. "Our access to the tree means any of us can lose our way. It is a hazard of the work we do. The Queens can only oversee so much, be it Black Queen Jan Xie heading up security and espionage, Black Queen Nielsen directing regional assignments, or our leader White Queen Greene supervising it all while he monitors our international relationships. Even then, the outer council of Rooks needs to grant approval, as a double check, even on our Queens."

"And now, because of William, even the Queen's Gambit will be scrutinized for everything they do?" Leah asked.

"William, Ian, and all the other Mystics that have gone astray. No one is above the eyes of the council. It is part of our checks and balances." Grace took a knee next to a small batch of wilted flowers. "Poor things grew too fast, before the foxgloves could fend off the deer." Grace placed her hand on the ground and shut her eyes.

A shiver ran up Leah's spine, and her arm grew hot. Asmodeus's voice bubbled up inside of her, whispering in her ear. *I don't like this. What is she doing?*

The flowers in front of Grace quivered. Stems that had previously slumped over stretched up to the sky, leaves broadened while new shoots sprang from the ground. Suddenly, the few dull pink flowers were now dozens of vibrant dahlias with blooms bigger than Leah's hands.

Gevurah. Asmodeus muttered in her ear.

Grace stood and brushed off her hands. "I've turned this garden into a little hobby of mine. I'm still getting used to the growing season, but I've still been able to keep this little patch of land going strong."

Leah looked around the garden, taking in the vibrant colors of each of the flowers. Grace had turned this empty clearing into a little paradise. The longer she looked, the more she saw. She watched as bees lazily flew in and out of black-eyed Susans, poppies, and marigolds. Squirrels darted between blueberry bushes, and birds swooped in from the trees to grab berries or catch a bug. Grace had created a beautiful little ecosystem.

"This is where I come to think. A little oasis from all the pain that the Infinity Board has put on me. Our work can help millions without them ever knowing, and yet it can also take a toll on us. On our minds and souls. I brought you here because I was like you once, angry and outspoken when a White Bishop came and tried to help me. She told me I wouldn't get anywhere fighting against the current.

Instead, she suggested a different way to harness my frustrations."

"And what was that? Grow flowers?" Leah asked.

Grace smirked and shook her head. "The flowers keep me centered. But the Bishop who spoke to me told me that there are some in the Infinity Board that want to reform it. They know that the change will be slow. Like-minded people need enough members in positions of power to make the concerted effort. We want the Infinity Board to be better. To *do* better. Outdated dogma dictates us. Even a few changes toward bringing the Board into the twenty-first century would help."

Leah huffed and clenched her jaw. "But the threat is already here, at our doorstep. And we still aren't doing anything to change. It's great that you have this vision of change, but how long is that going to take? Years? We don't have that kind of time."

Grace started back toward the river, her hands behind her back. "We've moved quickly in the past decade. That White Bishop I spoke of is no longer a Bishop but Black Queen Nielsen herself. And me, I've moved up the ranks faster than anyone else. It may be too slow for your standards, but change that comes with stability and through patience is better than a radical revolt coming from a Pawn that can do nothing but scream."

Leah walked up beside her. "So, what should I do then? Keep my mouth shut and behave like a good Pawn?"

"Perhaps. Maybe instead of butting heads with the leader, you focus on changing the minds of your fellow Pawns. Let me focus on Constance. We know the threat Legion has, and we all fear it as much as you do, even if we don't show that fear."

Leah contemplated Grace's words. Maybe progress had been made, but was it fast enough? Was it worth trying to change her peers' minds, instead of constantly angering those in a higher station?

They stood by the river and watched the water flow by. Then Grace said, "I presume you will share this conversation with Pawns Turner and O'Connor, but I would like it if you were to keep it between you three, for now. Some others in the Infinity Board grow weary when we speak of change, so I'd prefer this discussion be contained. Lead the other Pawns to see your way, but keep me out of it. After all, our focus must be on neutralizing Legion. Any distraction suggesting a systemic change will only slow this hunt."

Leah let it all sink in, feeling some relief at the fact that she was not alone. "We will keep this quiet for now."

Grace smiled. "Good. I knew I saw a lot of me in you. We could do great things together, you and I."

CHAPTER 17

SPAR INTO THE NIGHT

L eah wiped the sweat from her brow and looked across the sparring circle at Gabe. The Pawns had been practicing for the better half of the warm afternoon, and the sun was setting on the horizon. "One more time."

Sarah looked up to the sky. "Ugh! Come on. Sparring practice is over. Let's go eat. I'm starving."

Leah glanced around the field, watching Joanna stomp off toward the academy with Brandon trailing behind her. She met Ricardo's gaze as he smirked, flitting his eyes between her and Gabe. He helped Miranda up after having knocked her down from a particularly hard burst of *Malchut*. They followed behind the others toward the cafeteria for dinner.

Leah looked back at Gabe and readied her stance. "Go on ahead and eat without me, then. This jerk and I are gonna be out here all night if he doesn't actually fight."

Isaac raced up beside Sarah and pulled her toward the academy. "Come on. It's not our fault these two lovebirds want to wrestle some more."

"Hey, mind your business," Gabe said, his cheeks blushing as he let out a smirk at Isaac.

"I'm just saying, Sid told me they got ice cream on their grocery run. You know they'll run out of all the good stuff tonight."

"You hear that, Leah? Ice cream!" Sarah shouted, walking backward.

"I said go on ahead."

"Whatever. Your loss. I'll be sure they run all out of mint chocolate chip before you get a chance."

Leah looked back at Sarah and glared. "If you know what's good for you, you better save me some."

Sarah gave Leah a wink and a salute. "You got it! Have fun, lovebirds."

Isaac and Sarah waved them off and ran to join the others.

Gabe waved back at Isaac and locked eyes with Leah. "So, we're still doing this?"

Leah closed her fist and smiled. "And we'll keep doing it until you stop letting me win." She punched forward and let go a wave of *Malchut* that barreled across the field.

Gabe lifted his arms and took the brunt of the energy. It barely moved him, and Leah noted he used *Netzach* to keep in place.

Leah pushed herself forward, jumping off the ground and reeling up for a kick aimed directly at his head.

She was inches away when he clapped his hands, and all her momentum drained in an instant. She fell onto the ground next to him and swiped at his feet.

Gabe was faster, and he jumped away, releasing a *Malchut* push that sent Leah tumbling backward. She regained her balance and growled. "You're still holding back!"

She launched forward, sending punch after punch. She

knew her blows wouldn't kill him, but his counterattacks barely hurt. He held back too much, and it made it easy for her to close in.

Her third punch pushed him off balance and she lunged forward, ready to land a hit that would leave him dazed.

His fist met hers, and the impact of *Malchut* on *Malchut* sent her flying. She landed hard on her back while he stumbled to get up.

He wasn't playing anymore. It was about time.

She leaped at him again and reeled for a right hook, only to feign at the last second with her left. She released a small amount of *Malchut* to his ribs and he stumbled back, certain to have a decent bruise on his side come the next morning.

By sparring rules, it was over, and she'd won.

She smiled and brushed off the dirt, a huge grin on her face. "You're still too open," she said. "You've got to lower your arms and be ready for any—"

He shoved his knee into Leah's gut. *Malchut* followed suit, knocking the wind out of Leah as she went reeling through the air and landed on her side. She looked up at the darkening sky, feeling the world spinning.

Gabe raced over. "Leah! Oh geez, I'm sorry!"

"You cheated!" Leah said as breath came back into her lungs. "Of all people. You, Gabe. I can't believe it."

"I said I'm sorry. Here, I'll help you up." He reached out a hand. Leah grabbed it and smirked.

She swung up her leg and connected her foot to his stomach, pushing off with a little help from *Malchut*. She held on tight to his hand as the force cartwheeled him over her head and he landed, hard, on his back just above her.

All the air left his body, and through wheezes, Gabe said, "Good one."

Leah slapped his shoulder with the back of her hand

and smiled. "Not too bad yourself, cheater. Once you stopped treating me like I'm your girlfriend or something."

He didn't reply, and when Leah turned her head to look up at him, she saw him scratching his head. "Well . . . about that. What if we dated?"

Leah rolled up on her side and crawled next to him, placing a hand on his chest. Gabe wrapped his arms around her and pulled her in, letting out a deep sigh as she settled her head on his chest. She felt the heat emanating from him, and even though they were both sweaty from practice, it was comforting.

The guilt inside her bubbled back to the surface, the fear that she was letting her parents down. The fear that Gabe wasn't good enough.

Leah took a deep breath, the conversation with Sarah and Isaac replaying in her head.

You're not marrying him. You're only sixteen and deserve some happiness.

She pushed that guilt back down and shook her head. "No, let's not call it anything. Not yet at least. Not with everything going on." She slipped her hand into his and squeezed, feeling the warmth coming off his body.

He nodded. "I think I can handle that."

"Good, because I don't know if I could handle dating someone who cheats at sparring."

Gabe laughed. "Shut up."

They lay there, looking up at the sunset as the reds faded into purple and listening to the crickets, watching the stars twinkle to life as the remnants of the sun all but vanished.

"This is nice," Leah finally said.

"Yeah. It almost feels . . . normal."

Leah sighed. "Maybe one day soon we can make it official. We can sneak off and do what normal couples do. I dunno, find movies on the internet and eat popcorn."

Gabe picked up her hand, interlaced with his, and kissed the back of it. "Yeah, a little sparring, then a little movie while I ice my bruises."

Leah pushed herself up off the grass and looked at him. "That would be nice, wouldn't it?"

He nodded. "Yeah, I think so."

She leaned in and planted a kiss on his lips. He pressed into it, his teeth lightly grazing the bottom of her lip.

A few moments passed, and she pulled back and smiled. "I think so too."

CHAPTER 18

THE ORPHANAGE

When the orders came back from the Infinity Board, Sid and Grace called on the Pawns to suit up and ready themselves for the mission.

Minutes later, Leah stood in the armory, pocketing a loaded magazine and checking over her gun with the others. Her motions were second nature now, barely even paying attention as she tightened her tactical belt.

Rigel hadn't lied; his intel had been correct. Scouting Knights had confirmed multiple demons and at least twenty-two children. Luckily, intel suggested the children were not possessed, so the job was simple: rescue the kids and capture the demons. Given the magnitude of demons present, the orders clearly stated that the lives of the Mystics came first, so termination of a demon may be necessary.

Leah hated the way the Infinity Board glossed over the fact that they were just given orders to kill, but she loaded her gun anyway. At least this time, saving the children was the priority.

The ring of metal broke Leah's concentration as Isaac dropped his magazine, bullets rolling across the floor. She crouched next to him and reached for the magazine as he did. His hand shook, and when their hands met, she felt how cold it was. She let go and scooped up the loose bullets, offering them back to him.

"Everything alright?"

Isaac spoke in a quiet whisper, his eyes focused on the bullets as he put them in the clip one by one. "No. Everything's not alright."

Leah watched as the last of the team left the armory, leaving just the two of them behind. "What is it?" she asked.

"You've got to be bothered by it too, right? Knowing what we're going into?" Isaac said.

"You mean finally going on a rescue mission?"

Isaac shook his head. "Rescuing kids, yeah. But what about the others? Those orders seemed clear to me. Try to capture them but shoot to kill if it comes down to it. These bullets I'm loading, they're going to be the end for someone."

Numbness spread through Leah, and a cold sweat formed on her brow. "Maybe, maybe not. If we get the upper hand, if we can get in there undetected, then we can take them out before they see us. We're trained to do this. They're just demons."

"I know. I just have this feeling that something's going to go wrong."

"Better to save twenty some kids from possession, or whatever plans Legion has for them. We finally have a chance to do something major."

Isaac nodded and stood, sliding the magazine into his pistol. "I just don't want to forget that they are people too. Don't let me forget that."

Leah checked her belt one more time and turned to the exit. "I won't, and you do the same for me, okay?"

"Yeah, okay."

Rain pummeled the roof of the otherwise silent van. Grace pressed a few buttons on the GPS before looking at Eric. "Ten minutes out. We've lost contact with the scouts."

Eric gripped the steering wheel and looked in the rearview mirror at Leah before shooting a glance at Grace. "Lost contact? Are we still proceeding with the assignment?"

Grace eyed the GPS. "Yes. Just step on it." She looked back at Sarah, Leah, and Joanna. "You three ready for whatever happens?"

Leah glanced at Sarah and Joanna, clenching her jaw. "I'm ready."

She ran through the plan once more in her head. Surround the building, use *Tiferet* to get a visual, neutralize as many targets as possible with the tranquilizer snipers, and proceed inside to terminate any remaining threats. All done while Constance infiltrates and locates the children. But now, after losing the scouts, they might have lost that plan.

She eyed the silver car that drove by on the left. Constance shut off the headlights as she passed them, shrouding the car in darkness.

"Five minutes out. Proceed with the plan," Constance said in Leah's earpiece.

Leah rubbed her hands together, warming them while covering up the tremors. Isaac's instincts might be right after all, but she couldn't let the others know she was just as afraid.

After days of silence, Asmodeus sounded in her ear. *This is a war. There will be casualties.*

Leah looked into the rearview mirror. She knew no one else could hear him, but the panic was still the same.

She looked out the window, pressing her thumb into her palm as she muttered under her breath, "It doesn't make it any better."

The van came to a halt at the end of a street, the last row of lights burned out, and Eric said over the radio, "Team one, arrived at location."

"Team two, we've arrived," Nykima's voice sounded over the earpiece.

"Team Leader, in position and waiting," Constance said.

Eric looked to Grace and nodded, then without a word, everyone stepped out of the van. Leah pulled one of the gun cases from the back, following behind Eric.

They settled into position near the guardrail at the end of the street. The road dropped off to a busy highway below, then there it was, the fenced off orphanage nestled between a self-storage unit facility and a row of abandoned houses.

Grace, Joanna, and Sarah skirted off the road toward the overpass several hundred feet away.

A few minutes later, Leah heard Grace over the comms. "Team one in position."

Leah grabbed a pair of binoculars and homed in on the row of empty houses as Nykima and Brandon used *Malchut* to leap onto the roof. She turned her gaze to the storage facility and spotted Sid and Isaac setting up on the edge of the roof before she heard, "Team two in position."

Constance's voice sounded over the comms. "Any sign of the scouts?"

"Negative," Eric, Sid, Grace, and Nykima said in unison.

"Alright, proceed with scanning, then."

Leah felt the warmth build behind her eyes, and the world brightened as if the moon had shined three times brighter. The sea of cars below became a stream of golden light she had to turn away from.

She trained her eyes on the orphanage, her vision zooming in and drowning out the rest of the world around her.

At first, she thought the afterimage of the highway had impacted her vision, but the longer she looked, the more she realized she saw nothing. No movement, no shine, no entities within the two-story building surrounded by fencing.

Miranda was the first to speak. "No detection."

Followed by Ricardo. "No detection."

Joanna, Brandon, Sarah, and Isaac all repeated the same finding.

Leah pressed on her earpiece and spoke. "No detection."

Something is wrong. Stay alert, Asmodeus said.

"Team two, on my six," Constance said. "Proceed with caution. Team one, close in on target."

Eric rested the sniper rifle behind the guardrail and removed his pistol from its holster. Standing, he reached out a hand to Leah and pulled her toward the woods. Her vision still hadn't come back by the time they converged with Grace and her Pawns. They crossed the overpass together, Sarah, Joanna, and Leah guided by Eric and Grace. The bond between Leah and her uncle grew warm as they reached the fence, and Eric barreled through it like it was a sheet of paper, leaving behind a hole for everyone else to pass through.

They raced up to the orphanage's wall, and Grace unlocked the window and hopped inside. She turned, helping the others while Eric monitored the perimeter.

Leah blinked a few times inside the orphanage, her vision finally coming back as she pulled out a flashlight and surveyed what looked to be an office.

Leah and Eric headed left down the hall while Grace and the others went right. Glass broke above them, and Leah froze, looking at the ceiling.

"Inside the children's room," Constance said over the comms.

There was no sign of life as they proceeded through the house. They checked over the kitchen as Sid's voice sounded over the radio. "Basement's clear."

They found the stairs as Grace spoke. "First floor, clear."

"Nothing on the second floor," Nykima said.

Moments later, after they surveyed several more bedrooms, Eric said, "Nothing on the third floor."

The teams rendezvoused on the first floor living room, and Constance tossed a pile of clothes onto the couch. "Looks like they were just here. Whatever happened with the scouts must have tipped them off. I want a second round with *Tiferet*. I need confirmation no one is here."

"Yes, White Bishop!" Everyone said in unison. They broke away and shut off their flashlights, casting the house in complete darkness before each of their eyes glowed gold.

Leah headed up the stairs and to the second floor before she heard it. A familiar melody played in her ear, lulling her to its source. She froze on the top stair.

"Leah? Everything okay?" Isaac asked.

She looked back, releasing her grasp on *Tiferet* and seeing Isaac's blurred silhouette standing at the base of the staircase. "Yeah, I think. I just want to check something up here." Her eyes drifted to a door that she swore had been closed moments before.

The melody sounded again in her ears, a high tone that begged her to follow. She stepped into the room and flicked on her flashlight. It was small, with stacks of papers and books all over the floor and a desk in the corner.

"I already checked that room," Joanna said from behind her.

"Can't you hear that?" Leah asked, turning to speak with Joanna. But she wasn't there. Instead, she was already on her way down the steps.

The melody ate away at her ears, growing louder and louder, compelling Leah to move into the room.

I hear it, too. It sounds . . . familiar, Asmodeus said.

She stood in front of a bookcase, the song sounding from the other side. Her fingers moved along the shelves, caressing the books in front of her. She pushed past them, feeling at the back of the shelf paneling before her hand found a small lever.

Leah wrapped her fingers around it and pulled. The bookcase moved, held up by hinges anchored on the wall. She swallowed as she stepped through.

CHAPTER 19
HIDDEN SPACES

The song grew louder, calling Leah into the dark room. She trained her flashlight on the source. A small music box rested in the center of the space.

She stepped farther inside, and the floor creaked beneath her. The scent of mold filled her nostrils, and she moved her light, spotting several dusty couches and furniture.

The flashlight flickered out before it reached the corner of the room.

"It took you long enough."

The soft voice came from the dark corner. Leah reached for her gun. Her flashlight flickered back to life and trained on a bony hand wagging a finger at her.

"I wouldn't do that if I were you. Unless you want to end up like your friend here."

She looked to where the hand pointed and found a crumpled heap of flesh in a pool of blood. She made out an unfamiliar face and could only assume it was one of the missing scouts.

Two bright eyes appeared on what Leah first thought

was an empty sofa. She took her hand off her gun and took a step forward.

A woman sat in front of her, holding something in her lap.

That is no demon . . . Asmodeus's voice was strained, and the fear made Leah pause.

"What is it then?" she whispered.

An abomination.

The woman let out a shrill laugh. "Abomination? Me? And what does that make you, dead Kyjak?"

Leah's heart beat heavy in her chest. It could hear Asmodeus. She took a step back and held out a hand. "Look, I don't know what game you are playing, but there's a handful of other Mystics here. You might take down one or two, but no way you could defeat them all. Come quietly and we won't kill you."

The woman laughed, a raspy bestial sound that echoed off the walls. "I'm here to deliver a message. To you. Leah Ackerman."

"A message for me? From whom?"

The woman stood and stepped forward, light from the office behind Leah spilling onto her. She wore scrubs, appearing like a typical nurse Leah would have met at a hospital, if her glowing red eyes were replaced with brown eyes, curly brunette hair framing her seemingly normal face. In her hands, she carried a child, no older than four to five years old, emaciated and sleeping in her arms. The nurse held a kitchen knife up to the child's throat.

Leah gasped. "What are you—"

"Don't move."

Leah dropped her flashlight and curled her hands into fists. Anger boiled inside of her, forming a pressure inside her chest—*Malchut* begging to burst out.

The nurse tilted her head slightly and smiled. A void

grew in the woman's eyes as her face became emotionless and as still as a mannequin's.

Kill it! Asmodeus shouted in her head.

"Please," Leah said. "Let the child go."

Kill it now. The child is already lost. Kill it! Kill it! Kill it!

The nurse clicked her tongue. "Little weak Kyjak. So impatient. Don't you want to hear what Legion has to say?"

Leah gritted her teeth. "What is it?"

Her voice changed into something deeper and inhuman. "You've been lucky, Leah Ackerman. But if you continue down this path, a fate worse than death will follow. Everyone you've ever loved will die, and your parents will not be the only loss you mourn. Submit, or die."

The nurse raised the knife in a flash and brought it down on the child.

Time slowed; Leah's eyes followed the knife as it moved closer to the child's throat. She couldn't move. She wasn't fast enough. She stared in horror as the tip of the blade closed in.

Static sparked through the air, pulsing from behind her. At that moment, the blade froze centimeters away from the child's neck.

Leah pushed against the sensation of static, a feeling like moving through gelatinous liquid, and saw Isaac, hands clapped together, signifying *Hod.*

She smirked and turned back to the nurse, using *Malchut* to propel herself forward. Leah landed a punch square on the nurse's chest, breaking her from her hold on the child. The child collapsed to the ground as the nurse went flying back.

Isaac sprung forward, scooping the child up in his arms. "Do you think he's . . . ?"

Leah focused on Isaac and shook her head. "He'll be okay, he has to."

Isaac nodded, then focused on something past Leah, his eyes widening.

Leah took the hint and braced herself a split second before the nurse careened into her.

In an instant, the nurse was on top of her, knife in hand. The blade edged forward, slipping closer and closer to Leah's chest.

A loud bang rang in Leah's ears.

The nurse's head jerked back, blood splattering the wall behind her. She collapsed backward as Leah crawled away, peeling her eyes away from the dead nurse.

"Leah!" Isaac shouted behind her.

A soft red glow started spreading from the wound in the nurse's head. Blood moved of its own accord, tracing symbols on the floor and scaling incomprehensibly up the walls and onto the ceiling. Patterns of familiar lines and circles traced around the room in an instant, the red glow brightening.

Get out! Now! Asmodeus screamed from inside her head.

Leah stumbled to her feet and turned to Isaac, racing forward and pushing him backward.

He shoved back and shook his head.

"Isaac! What are you doing?"

"The kid! We need to save the kid!"

Pain seared through Leah's body, and the red glow pulsed. She let go of Isaac, clutching at her head as the pain bore into her skull.

The pulsing light grew brighter and brighter as Isaac picked up the kid. He turned and looked at Leah before falling to his knees.

Leah crawled toward them, the pain pounding through

her body as she grabbed on to Isaac. She pulled, but he didn't move.

His eyes filled with red light, and his mouth opened in a silent scream.

The floor shook, and red energy crackled in the air. It accumulated around the nurse's body, and it felt as if gravity itself shifted toward the corpse.

Not like this! Hold on to him! Asmodeus said.

Leah's left arm moved against her will. She held on tight to Isaac with her other hand as a pulse of force thrust them backward, toward the exit.

They barely moved, the pull from the nurse's corpse too strong.

I need more. Give me more.

Leah didn't know what else to do. She let him in. Let him take what he needed. Energy surged through her, voices shouting and screaming in her ears. The world around her undulated, and a sickness spread into every inch of her body. Pressure built in her arm, compacting more and more until it felt like her skin was tearing apart.

Then it released.

They flew. Her clutch on Isaac and the child remained tight, even through the pain. Their bodies flew through the door and into the office, her back slamming into the wall. The last thing she saw was the faint red glow in Isaac's eyes fading away into darkness.

POSSESSED

Water lapped at Leah's ankles as she came to her senses. She stood in the vast sea of darkness, the only light coming from some unseen place above her.

In the distance ahead, a second beam of light shone on a white marble table, cast on its side. Something else leaned against it, a dark and crumpled mass.

She raced forward as the mass turned into a silhouette, and soon enough she could make out the features of Asmodeus's pale body propped up against the table. A thick black substance oozed from an open wound stretching up the entirety of his left arm.

She should've hated him, been revolted by him, and been happy that this had happened. Yet, she couldn't. Her heart pained, and she raced to his side to assess the wound.

It looked more like a heap of discolored ground meat, and she was certain she could see bone. "Asmodeus, can you hear me? I'm here," Leah yelled.

A shallow, whispering voice sounded from behind him. "I told you we had to leave."

"I . . . I couldn't leave them."

"We almost died because of it." Asmodeus shifted his head and opened his eyes. Where they had been dark and menacing before, they were dull gray with a tiny spark of light in the center that looked back at her. "Legion will doom this world, and we will both lose our people. We cannot take another hit like that."

"But we saved them. You saved them. Isaac and the kid."

Asmodeus shut his eyes and breathed in. The light above flickered, and the wound on his arm quivered. The black ooze seemed to stop leaking altogether. "I need time to heal. We didn't die, and your friend is safe. Perhaps a clearer mind might see that as a win."

"Sorry. I didn't think—"

"I cannot blame you for protecting your people. This feeling you have. This . . . humanity . . . is strong."

Leah felt a pull in the pit of her stomach, a sensation coated in fear that wasn't her own. *Eric.*

The waters lapping at her ankles pulled at Leah, sinking her. "I have to go. What can I do?"

Asmodeus held up his right hand and snapped his fingers. The white table slowly transformed, melting underneath him and reshaping into a small chair that lifted him out of the water. "Nothing. This will heal in time. Until then, I must rest. Please don't do anything brash."

His body became as still as stone, and the light above them flickered out, casting her back into darkness.

Leah groaned as she opened her eyes to a swinging pendant lamp that hung from the ceiling, illuminating the office. Her back ached, and she was certain bruises covered it all the way down, at the very least. She propped herself up on her elbows and spotted both Isaac and the child just out of arm's reach on her right.

She worked her jaw and whispered, "Isaac, are you okay?" Leah turned and crawled on her elbows closer to him. "Isaac?"

She could hear the others closing in, footsteps sounding on the stairs just outside the door.

Leah grabbed his bulletproof vest and shook, shouting his name. Then she saw it—dark veins snaking their way up his neck and onto his cheeks, and a blue hue encircling his eyes. Her hand brushed his face, and all she felt was cold.

"No. Isaac, no. No, no, no!" She shook him.

The steps reached the door, and a voice sounded behind her. "Leah, what's going on? Knights get on the perimeter! What was that sound?"

Eric and Nykima entered the room, their guns sweeping the room. Nykima peered into the entrance, then shouted, "Clear!"

Constance stepped in and knelt beside Leah, resting a hand on her shoulder, pulling her back from Isaac's body. "Let me have a look."

She traced her fingers around Isaac's face and crooned.

"Isaac!" Sarah shouted from behind Leah.

Constance's grip on Leah's shoulder tightened, and she yanked Leah back as she stood. "Everyone, keep away from the body." She clicked her earpiece. "Sid, come to the upper floor. Now!" Constance pulled Leah up to her feet and back away from Isaac before looking her in the eye. "What happened here?"

Leah looked over at the entrance behind the bookcase. "It was a trap. There was a demon in there, holding a knife to a kid's throat. She claimed she had a message for me. We tried to stop her. Isaac used *Hod*, and I knocked her back, but she caught me off guard. He shot her, and that triggered a ritual."

Ricardo started toward the entrance to the secret room, but Constance spoke in a booming voice. "No one enters that room."

Nykima pulled the child away from Isaac. "He's still breathing. No signs of any similar affliction to Pawn O'Conner."

Sid came rushing into the room and took a knee next to Isaac, ripping open Isaac's bulletproof vest and swiftly cutting his long-sleeved shirt open with his knife.

The black marks that followed his veins were thicker below the neck, and even worse around his stomach.

Sid rested a hand on Isaac's stomach and closed his eyes. He instantly flung his hand off Isaac's body as something moved just beneath the surface of his skin. "It's a possession alright, but not one I've seen before."

Constance stared at Isaac like a hawk. "Neither have I."

"What does that mean? Can you save him?" Leah asked.

"Can you carry him?" Constance asked Sid.

Sid nodded.

Constance continued, "Grace, notify the Infinity Board. We need to take him back to the academy at once."

Grace cleared her throat and stepped out of the room.

Sid's eyes glowed yellow. "We won't get there in time. His body is already shutting down."

"No! We have to do something. We can take him to a hospital," Sarah said, struggling against Gabe as she tried stepping toward Isaac.

Grace stood in the doorway. "Hospitals without Mystics wouldn't know what to do with him. The closest one we could get to is three hours away. I just received confirmation. Is that close enough?"

"No," Sid said.

Eric cleared his throat. "What about the others?"

"What *others*?" Constance asked.

"There's an old Druid camp nearby. They might not be there, but they'd know we're coming. It's worth a shot."

Nykima shook her head. "We don't have any treaties with the Druids. They won't help us."

"Do you have a better solution?" Eric snapped back.

Nykima didn't say another word, and the room fell silent.

Constance pinched the bridge of her nose. "Fine. Eric, take Sid and Isaac to the Druids. Leah too. She has my permission to give any information about this ritual to them."

"I'm going too!" Sarah shouted.

"You will do as you're told," Grace said, shooting her a glare.

Sid looked at Sarah for a moment, then Grace. "Actually, we could use the help. Gabe, Leah, and Sarah should be enough to help me. We'll need those closest to Isaac to perform *Chesed*."

Grace nodded. "Very well. Let's move out. You've got a Pawn to save."

CHAPTER 21

CHESED

Eric had moved the van outside the orphanage's front doors by the time Gabe and Sid carried Isaac down. They'd fashioned a stretcher together with loose bookshelves and torn curtains to not touch him as they carried him.

Leah helped Sarah put down the back seats before Sid slid Isaac into the back. He jumped in beside Isaac and looked at Leah and Sarah. "I need you two back here with me. Gabe, you can take the front passenger. Just be ready for instruction."

Constance and Gabe closed the back doors before Constance rounded to the driver's side and eyed Eric. "Keep us posted. If anything goes wrong, pull out. No one else is getting hurt tonight. You understand?"

Eric nodded, and she tapped on the car's roof. Eric hit the gas, leaving Constance and the others behind.

Streetlights raced overhead, illuminating Sid as he repositioned himself to cradle Isaac's head in his lap. He rested his palms on either side of Isaac's head and shut his eyes.

"Should only take thirty minutes, tops," Eric said as he merged onto the highway.

"He can't wait that long!" Sid said. Speed if you can."

Leah's head rocked back as Eric floored it and said, "Better hope there aren't any cops out."

Sid opened his eyes and looked at Leah, then Sarah. "How's your knowledge of *Chesed*?"

Sarah took in a breath and looked down at Isaac. "We've never done it, but it's the healing one, right?"

Sid nodded. "I'll take the lead. Gabe, you wait until I ask you to join in. Leah and Sarah, all you two need to do is think of happy memories. Preferably between you and Isaac. You'll feel me link up with those memories. The healing comes from that love, that joy, from the moments you've had together. Once it gets going, hold on to the memories as best you can. You should be able to feel what I'm doing. Don't fight that. Just let me guide you in sending that energy into him."

They both nodded, and Sid lowered his head, closing his eyes and rubbing his hands together. The van's temperature grew warm, a gentle heat that lulled Leah and relaxed her shoulders.

Sarah met Leah's eyes, and they both hovered their hands above Isaac, interlocking their fingers with each other before closing their eyes.

Leah rifled through her memories of Isaac, remembering Sarah and him showing up at the car door window on her first day at the outpost. She recalled his enormous eyes staring in at her with a bowl of food in his hands. A soothing warmth trickled down from her head and to her fingertips.

With the thoughts flowing, she sensed Sid's energy grabbing hold of her thoughts and pooling them into Isaac.

Opening her eyes, she saw the bright golden light flowing down her arms and streaming into him, flowing into Isaac through his temples. When she closed her eyes again, her thoughts intermixed with Sarah's, and she saw moments Sarah had shared with Isaac. Their first days at the Outpost, when Sarah took him under her wing and made him her friend.

The memories flowed out of them and down into Isaac's body, filling him. The moment it touched him, her memory seemed to pull away. She strained against it, holding the memory in her mind's eye, but the more she held on, the more it pulled away.

Other thoughts filled her mind. The fear of losing him the moment he left her to face Asmodeus alone, and the pain of seeing him on the floor with blackened veins.

Happiness dissolved in an instant, and the warm glow of energy turned into a dark black void. She was alone. Useless. Weak. How could she ever think that they could save Isaac? He was going to die right in front of her while she waved her hands like an idiot.

Her body grew weaker by the second. Nothing mattered, and the pain she felt on the outside was only a poor reflection of what she felt inside. She opened her eyes and saw Isaac's pale body. The blackened veins seemed to grow bigger, and his body jerked left and right.

She looked at Sid, who clenched his eyes tight, sweat beading at his temples.

Leah struggled to take in a breath. Isaac was going to die. She looked up at Sarah, whose hands fell at her sides as tears poured down her face.

The car swerved hard and came to a full stop, jostling them around.

"Sid! Stop!" Eric shouted.

Isaac gasped, opening his eyes for a moment before his head slumped to one side.

The despair slithered away from Leah's mind, and the dark shadow looming over her brightened. The icy cold that bored into her vanished, and she took in a full, deep breath.

Sid pulled his hands away from Isaac and looked around the van. "I . . . I'm sorry. I overextended. He was so close to dying."

Eric shook his head and took the exit off the highway. "It's fine. But maybe hold off for a bit if you can. He's breathing again, and we're almost there."

Sarah rubbed her arms and glanced up at Leah. "What was that? Those thoughts. I couldn't hold on to a happy memory. It was just . . . dark."

Sid sat up and wiped the sweat from his brow. "I'm sorry, that was my fault. *Chesed* drains quickly and delves into its counterpart, *Agshekeloh*, easily. I've done it enough that I know my limits, but I couldn't stop. Not yet."

Leah looked down at Isaac, watching his chest rise and fall. "He's breathing. That's all that matters."

Sid looked down and rested a hand on him. "They all wanted him to go with Black Queen Jan Xie, you know. All the other Knights and Bishops."

Leah narrowed her eyes. "What? Why?"

"They didn't see what I could see in him."

Sarah patted Isaac's leg. "Same as me then, I guess. If it hadn't been for Grace."

Sid shook his head. "They fought over you, and Grace had the last call. Isaac showed great proficiency in weapons. He scored low on the trials, which made him a perfect candidate for her program. His skill with *Hod* was unmatched, though. Still, the others didn't want to see that. Glad I did, or else I wouldn't have truly seen what he's capable of."

"And what's that?" Leah asked.

"A bird flew into my office window one day. I didn't know what it was at first, but when I came to the window and looked down onto the greens below, there was Isaac cradling a Blue Jay. It'd fallen two stories, and I assumed the poor thing was lost. Then I felt it. When you use *Tiferet* enough, you can sometimes feel stronger energy without it, and what he was doing felt like sticking my finger in an electrical socket. It was gone the moment I felt it, and the bird simply flew away. It happens, from time to time, spikes in energy, but for him to show that kind of compassion, and have that much energy before bonding . . . That's what I believe we need more of in our Mystics."

Eric cleared his throat and looked in the rearview mirror. "We're almost there. You three just follow me and Sid's lead, okay? Druids like to use your words against you. It'll be better if you say nothing at all."

"So, do we bring weapons or not?" Gabe asked.

Eric shook his head. "There wouldn't be a point. They already know we're coming. They're clairvoyant, always ten steps ahead. We're coming to them for help. Hopefully, they've already agreed, and the agreement to be made is something they'd be interested in."

CHAPTER 22
DRUIDS

He slowed and turned onto a dirt path, branches scratching and brushing on the sides and top of the van as they traveled deeper into the woods.

A pain echoed inside Leah—a feeling that wasn't her own. She traced it back to Eric, sensing a twinge of regret as his eyes locked onto the path ahead.

After a couple of minutes, Eric slowed the van. "There he is."

Leah looked out the windshield and made out a figure in a long dark cloak holding up a lantern. Even as Eric pulled up to the cloaked figure and rolled down his window, Leah couldn't see their face behind the dark hood.

A tattooed hand, with dark bands and swirling symbols, reached out and rested on the side of Eric's face, placing a thumb on his forehead. A whisper spoke from under the hood. "Why have you come back?"

Eric shifted in his seat and reached out to the cloaked figure, his hand disappearing into the hood. "I come by no decision, but by the will of fate, and I hope to leave by the same means."

"Eric Mizrahi, you remember the ways well. Bring the others and follow me."

Eric killed the engine and turned to the others. "Leave everything behind. *Everything.*" He unbuckled and hopped out of the van.

Sid and Gabe pulled Isaac, still lying on the makeshift stretcher, from the van while Sarah and Leah followed close behind Eric.

The cloaked figure led them deeper into the woods, the smell of moss and wet leaves filling Leah's nose. Humidity hung heavier in the air more than she'd expected, and soon enough, they walked into a dense fog.

They all followed the light, a small beacon in an otherwise pitch-black abyss. Leah wondered how far away from the van they were when the fog cleared ahead of them and they came to a large circular tent with a lantern hanging out front.

Leah had seen tents like these before—yurts, as some called them—but nothing as fancy as this. It was large, with a canvas that stretched around poles that crossed back and forth, holding the structure in place.

Two people stepped out from behind a canvas door, carrying a handmade stretcher. The cloaked figure turned and faced Sid. "Place your sick one here. That thing you have him on is about to give."

Sid and Gabe moved Isaac over the makeshift stretcher, and in that instant, the binding broke free. They pulled his haphazard stretcher free and lowered him onto the new one.

The cloaked figures lifted the new stretcher and continued, moving past the yurt.

Other tents lined down the path ahead. Some were yurts like the one they'd first seen, while others were modern nylon ones. It almost looked like a bunch of contemporary travelers had crashed a medieval renaissance fair. Leah watched how people stepped out of the tents, watching in silence as they passed by.

Not all wore cloaks, either. Some had dressed in modern clothes; others wore what looked like furs. Many had the same blue tattoos that lined their faces and arms, illuminated by the lanterns that each hung outside their homes.

A voice, barely even a whisper, spoke in Leah's mind. *I don't like this place.*

"You're awake?" She muttered under her breath.

Be vigilant. I dislike it here.

The feeling was mutual, as her stomach tied itself in knots the farther down the path she went.

They stopped at the end of the dirt path, in front of a massive tent, nearly twice the size of all the others. As they all stepped in, one by one, Leah smelt something strange. Like an herb she couldn't quite place, but not one she'd ever want to cook with.

They walked to the center of the room, where the embers of a fire glowed. Leah looked up, seeing the small hole in the center of the canvas roof, the stars shining down on her.

The cloaked man gestured to the cushions around the fire. "Please, sit, and place the boy in front of me."

Leah took a seat next to Eric, as close as she could be to Isaac without the fire pit blocking her view. Sarah sat across from her, between Gabe and Sid.

Once settled in, the cloaked man pulled back his hood, revealing a weathered face and long gray hair tied back in braids. His beard obscured some of the faint blue tattoos that covered his face. "Eric Mizrahi. We have seen many moons come and go since we last saw you."

"Chief Cían, thank you for seeing us."

"Those moons did not pass without loss. She was a

warrior who did what was necessary, and now all we can offer is our condolences."

A pain rang in Leah's chest. She traced it back to Eric, who stared into the fire, jaw clenched.

Jade.

The chief continued, "Given what you've done for us, our people will not hide from you. We knew you'd come, but I'm afraid we can't help you with your request."

The knots in Leah's stomach grew tighter, and she dug her nails into her fists. Eric shook his head. "Please, Chief. One of our own was wounded. Possessed. But it's different. Strange. And we don't think we'll be able to save him without your help."

Cían waved a hand. "We know this. He obscures our visions the moment we knew you'd bring him. He carries a demon. And you are right to say that his affliction is different. Our sight is not completely useless around this one, suggesting that this possession is incomplete, the ritual severed in the middle of the process."

Sarah huffed and looked at Cían. "So, you know what happened? Then you can save—"

A glare from Eric shut her up. Sarah's gaze fell back onto the fire, and she pursed her lips.

The old man ignored her, instead turning to look at the door before another cloaked figure stepped into the room, carrying a glass bottle with a cork. The figure knelt beside Isaac. And waited.

Cían took in a breath. "We cannot see everything surrounding this boy, but this should tell us a little more."

The cork popped off the bottle, and almost immediately, an odor of fresh fruit, peat moss, and a sharp, putrid sting like hand sanitizer mixed with rotten eggs assaulted Leah's senses. She immediately covered her mouth and nose with one hand and leaned back from the concoction.

As she did so, Isaac hissed and twisted his body, turning his head left and right away from the bottle.

Leah looked at Sarah and then the others, who all stared at Isaac. They watched as he writhed about, but the smell affected none of them.

The cork slid back into the bottle, and the smell faded away. Leah gulped in clean air, clearing her nose from that volatile odor.

Sid tilted his head toward the bottle. "Mandrake? I've read that you've used it to stave off demons, but this . . . was it a concentrated form? How did you get past the . . ."

Leah watched the chief, who ignored Sid, instead staring directly at her. He waved off Sid and nodded his head to Leah. "I would like to speak with this one. Alone."

CHAPTER 23
THE CHIEF

Eric rose to his feet. "No! I came for you to help treat this boy. You need to talk to someone? Talk to me. Do you forget what I did for your people?"

Cían stood, flaring his nostrils. "Your little soldier suffers from a possession we haven't seen before. We haven't forgotten what you've done for us, but his reaction to the mandrake was volatile, suggesting that his time is nearly up. That demon is stuck between worlds and draining that boy of his vital life. Without our help, he will die. With our help, the demon could lure us into its trap. So, by all means, continue to argue with me and let him die, or grant me the right to speak to this one in private."

Sid pushed up from the pillowed seats and took a half bow. "With all due respect, Chief Cían, we are running out of time. Please, I implore you to—"

The Bishop's words halted the moment several figures in white and gray cloaks entered the room and stood beside Cían. "These are our best when it comes to matters of demons. They will stabilize him while I speak with this one."

Leah was the last to stand. Her heart raced in her chest.

Asmodeus's voice was a quiet one, repeating in the back of her mind. *He knows. He knows. Run! Get out.*

She looked at Gabe, who rubbed his thumbs into his palms and shook his head, a warning for her to not to go through with it.

Leah tore her gaze away. She had to do anything to save Isaac. "Uncle, let me speak to him. Isaac needs help. I won't make any deal I can't pay."

You're risking us. Risking me.

Eric let out a huff, placing his hands on his hips. "Fine."

"We've settled it then. The rest of you wait here while your soldier is being treated. Leah, if you would join me."

Anger and frustration echoed through the bond. She looked at Eric and did everything she could to send back reassurance and hope.

Eric leaned in close to her ear. "Remember, ten steps ahead. Be very careful with what you say and do."

Leah followed the man as he walked across the circular room and through the hanging curtains. Beyond was a hallway that connected the tent to another. He pulled back the curtain to reveal a small and dimly lit room with a low, round table and an assortment of green and gold cushions around it. The walls had an extra layer of curtains, dark blues and blacks that hung from the ceiling and draped to the sides.

As she stepped inside, heat washed over her with the faint scent of incense lingering in the air.

The chief gestured to the cushions. "Please, sit."

As Leah walked around the table and found herself directly across from him, Cían settled into the cushions, locating a plate and cone-shaped incense that he lit and set on the table.

Leah prepared herself for another assault on her senses. Instead, when the smell hit her, it arrived as a floral note that reminded her of her mother's perfume. The aroma calmed her, releasing the tension she had in her shoulders. "So, what's this about?"

The old man smiled, showing off a set of yellowed teeth interspersed with gold ones. "I suspect you already know. But that's the irony of it, me suspecting that is. You're an anomaly."

"Why would you say that?"

Cían smirked and looked down at the ribbon of incense smoke rising off the cone. He rubbed his hands together, humming a soft melody. "Only your friend Isaac hid from my vision of your arrival. Yet, you did something I couldn't predict. You are not fully connected to this plane." He tapped his finger in the air, pointing at her as he clicked his tongue. "There's something else inside you."

Leah's arm twitched, and sweat formed on her brow. "I . . . I . . ."

Cían reached across the table and grabbed her hand, his grip strong, and the heat emanating from his palm was unnaturally hot. "I know now that something lies within you, something that only relates to these demons. Whatever it is, though, is weak, or perhaps the thing is not fighting you for possession yet. If it were, the solution that was uncorked under your friend's nose would have been worse for you. And even now, you breathe in smoke meant to stun a demon into silence and hold my hand covered in oils meant to burn the possessed."

Leah yanked her hand away, rubbing her palm. Words wouldn't come out. She simply sat there, glaring at the man.

He leaned back and rested his hands on his lap. "I take it none of the other Mystics know about this. Perhaps that other young woman. Sarah, is it? She plays a part in your secret."

Leah crossed her arms, eyeing the exit behind Cían. "Why do you care?"

He shrugged. "It sparks my curiosity. You're an anomaly in more ways than one, and yet you are still *you*."

He's probing for information. He'll trick you to give it away freely, Asmodeus said.

Leah raised her eyebrow and smiled. "You want to know what it is? I'll tell you, but only if you help my friend."

Cían let out a laugh. "You bargain too little, and at the risk of losing too much."

"You knew we'd come, but you won't help us. Why even welcome us inside if you were only going to turn us away?"

He nodded. "We remained here, curious of what might drive Eric back here. He left under such dire circumstances, and we weren't sure if he would ever return. Yet, nothing has been offered to protect our kin, so no bargain is yet to be made."

"Do you even know what's going on outside your little commune? People are dying, being sacrificed all over the country. And now they're coming after us for trying to stop them."

Cían raised a finger. "People die every day, and cults come and go. Our interference has always cost us our blood. We watch and bargain to ensure payment comes as no surprise. This time, our bargain is not with the Infinity Board but with you."

Leah's head flinched back. "With me? Why me?"

He turned and held out a hand behind him. At that moment, a small child pulled back the curtain, holding a small teapot. Cían took it from him in one swift move and pulled the curtain back into place.

Cían grabbed two teacups from underneath the table and set them down. "We shall make this bargain over tea."

"Tea? You've tested me twice already. There's no way that's just tea."

Cían shrugged. "It is tea, technically. But not the kind you sip for pleasure, like an Earl Grey you'd have in the middle of the day. This is something more . . . impactful."

"Look, I want you to help my friend before it's too late. That's my only term. What are yours?"

He ignored her, instead looking down and pouring a dark green, steaming substance out of the teapot and into the cups. "Let me be clear. I'll be setting the terms, not you. First, if you refuse to drink this, then all bargains are off, and I will order you all to leave. That includes your friend, who may not make it through the night. However, drink it, and helping him will remain on the table."

Leah pulled one cup closer to her, breathing in a potent scent of mint and pine.

At least it doesn't pain me to breathe, Asmodeus murmured.

Leah looked up from the cup. "What's in it?"

The chief lifted it and breathed it in. "It is a simple potion. One we rarely share, and one you must never decline. It links us together for a short while. In that time, it will let me see your past, present, and potential future that lies ahead of you. Only then will I know the path you plan to take."

Leah copied him, breathing in the steam, hoping Asmodeus got the hint.

I don't detect any mandrake or other substances that would harm us.

She lifted the glass and chewed on her lip.

Cían smirked, his blue tattoos distorting under his wrinkled flesh. "You have no more questions?"

Leah finished the drink in one gulp. Earthy, bitter

flavors filled the back of her throat while mint settled on her tongue.

"I suppose not," Cían said, lifting his glass. "Salud." He followed her lead and downed his drink in one gulp.

"Now what?"

Cían reached under the table and pulled out another incense cone and lit it, releasing a thick cloud of red smoke that quickly filled the room.

He leaned back behind the curtain of smoke and said, "Now, we watch."

CHAPTER 24

MIST

Clouds of red smoke curled around Leah, taking shape and toiling with her senses. For a moment, she swore Cían had loomed over her, wearing his hooded cloak again and holding up a lantern. As soon as Leah was about to ask what he was doing, the rest of the red smoke took shape and transformed into a starless night.

Cían waved his hand and whispered, "Eric Mizrahi, follow me."

As Cían turned, the red mist consumed him.

Leah moved her head left and right, peering into a dense forest. She focused on a tiny figure in the distance. Small and childlike.

Leah pushed herself up from the ground, brushing off leaves and sticks before chasing after Cían. The earth moved faster than it should, and within two paces, she stood behind the child. Leah lightly pulled on their shoulder, but as the kid turned, the nameless Indian woman stared up at her. She collapsed to the ground, her eyes white as she felt at the gash in her stomach.

Leah knelt beside her, reaching for her arm, but she vanished, consumed by a red mist.

The world around her shifted. Trees rushed in, forming flat wooden walls. Treetops fell and formed a slanted roof. Dirt and leaves changed to floorboards. Leah looked down and saw the kid they'd saved back in her own arms. She stared at Isaac, intuition kicking in, and threw the kid toward her friend, just like she had done before. The nurse barreled into her at the last second, her knife inching toward Leah's chest.

A gunshot rang in her ears, followed by the nurse's head snapping back, blood splattering the walls behind her.

Time ticked by slowly, and Leah knew if she turned, she'd see Isaac there, still holding his gun. Instead, she transfixed her eyes on the blood moving along the walls as if it were alive. The room glowed, and the nurse's body shifted. It cracked once before silvery fingers tore out of her chest.

The creature moved like liquid metal, tearing free from the nurse's corpse, its long metallic arms wrenching its torso from hers. Once free, it twitched its head, with small black gouges for eyes and no nose or mouth, looking left and right until it settled on something behind Leah.

It skittered across the floor, crawling unnaturally toward Isaac. The thing leaped from the ground, clawing at his chest, digging its way in.

Leah reached for Isaac, trying to grab him and stop the thing from boring its way into him. Her hand grazed his arm, and the world around her shattered into millions of pieces.

She fell into a void of red mist before landing hard on the earth. Long grass sprouted up around Leah, and mud caked her hands. She stood up in a field, surrounded by others she immediately recognized as Pawns, Bishops, and Knights by their uniforms.

Fire burst from the hands of a female Knight beside her. She was dark-skinned, bearing a white emblem that signified her as a White Knight. Her eyes shone gold, and she pulled Leah up from the ground.

"They're coming!" The unfamiliar Knight yelled, flinging streams of fire into the tree line.

Leah followed the fire and found others racing toward them, wearing the same whites and blacks as them. Other Infinity Board members racing toward them.

"What's happening?" Leah shouted.

The earth shook, and roots shot up through the ground, piercing through several Knights and Pawns ahead of her. The roots raced toward her, and the unfamiliar Knight used *Malchut* to tear the roots to shreds.

Leah was in the middle of a battle between Mystics. A civil war.

The Knight who helped her flew backward, slammed by a *Malchut* blow, leaving Leah alone in front of the enemy. Energy flowed into her arms, readying herself for *Malchut*.

She took aim at the oncoming attack, but red mist crept up from the ground and obscured her vision. The world changed again, the squishy field beneath her turning into solid ground, and an old beat-up house closing in around her.

Her *Malchut* released against her will, firing bullets directly at the twisted body of her father.

"No," Leah whispered, her voice cracking, and she turned away from her father's corpse.

Her eyes fell on Alma, propped up against the wall, metal spikes piercing her body. Leah raced to her side.

"I'm sorry I let you down," Leah said.

Words muffled in Leah's ears as her eyes raced over

Alma's face. She was here again. She could save her, but she was a novice at *Chesed*. If only she could . . .

Alma's last words fell from her mouth. "You were brave. But remember that bravery comes at a price. Make sure you're . . . willing . . . to pay it." Her eyes dulled and a slight smile twitched on her face before going slack and lifeless.

Tears fell down Leah's face as she looked down at her dead mentor once again. Did she make her proud? Is this the path Alma would have wanted? Leah closed her eyes tight, the pain in her chest building and tightening.

When she opened them again, she stood on a slab of cement outside on a rainy day. Her left arm ached, and when she looked at it, black smoke bubbled off it. The longer she looked, the more skeletal it became. She traced it down to her elongated sharp claws. Sharp nails grazed her hard and stony palm as she opened and closed it. Her right hand was still her own. Still human.

Scotch and cigar smoke filled her senses, and the world turned again. Leah stood in an old office, before a brilliant silhouette of light. Rage tore through her body, a hatred beyond anything Leah had felt before. Involuntarily, she lunged at the light, and it engulfed her.

The light faded away, and she looked at her hands again. They were still human but no longer her own. She stared at the gold wedding band and the blond knuckle hairs. A lump formed in her throat as her eyes fell on the watch, and she realized this was her father.

Something else moved her, and Leah turned and rested against the corner of a dark room. Anger filled every fiber of her being, a rage that seethed between gritted teeth.

It felt like an eternity. Then a door behind her opened. "Mom? Dad? Are you guys home?" a familiar voice sounded in the dark.

It was Leah herself speaking. She waited until she saw

herself standing in the archway into the kitchen. Her heart pounded in her ears as the horrors of that night unfolded, not from her perspective, but from *his*. From Asmodeus. The words coming out of her mouth again, her fear, her confusion. She felt the scratching pain in her throat as the voice of her father came through her. Then the explosion, and everything went dark.

She stared at her father in the mirror, already emaciated and pale. He knew what to do. She had to die. A twisted smile shone on the mirror as he thought of how he could use this body to get close. Then it could be done. He'd have his revenge on the Mizrahis, and his debt to Legion would finally be over.

No. Enough of this, Asmodeus's voice bore through her mind.

Energy rippled through her arm, and something yanked Leah from behind. Everything in front of her blurred into a red mist, writhing and undulating around her. Bile rose in the back of her throat, and she thought she was going to throw up when the mist froze, settling into place.

She stared at Cían, sitting on his wooden throne. She lifted her hands, noting the sudden transparency before bringing her attention back to Cían.

He nodded at the two cloaked figures. "We must remain here another day. If the vision holds true, then our visitors will arrive by nightfall."

One of the cloaked figures shook their head. "You're risking the entire community on the whim that they will help. They won't care about Aengus. The longer we wait, the more he is lost to us."

Cían slammed his fist down. "He is my grandson! Those who can see know that this is the only chance we have. The only chance to still save him."

As the room fell silent, it faded away in another torrent

of red mist. Another second passed, and Leah stood on a rocky beach next to a small boy throwing rocks at the lake, the sky shades of reds and purples.

Movement broke free from the tree line, and the boy picked up another rock. "I knew you were coming, Grandpa. You don't have to hide."

Cían stepped out from the trees and lowered his hood, smiling at the boy. "You're getting better at that. Soon enough, I might have to step down."

Leah looked at the kid standing next to her. He had short ginger hair, and a birthmark stretched across his cheek.

"That's not why you came here, though," the boy said.

Cían nodded. "You shouldn't be wandering out this far. Your mother will be worried."

A voice, Cían's voice, tore through the vision, shouting at the top of his lungs, "No!"

Bright red light filled Leah's vision, and she tumbled back, falling onto her backside.

She opened her eyes and found herself sitting back on the cushions inside the small circular building. The smoke had cleared, and her eyes met Cían's across the table. He was breathing hard while glaring at her.

"Not even my own people have been able to reverse the visions of me before." His breathing slowed and he raised an eyebrow. "You are very interesting indeed, Leah Ackerman."

Leah looked down at the table. "What were those?"

"Visions of the past, mostly. And possibilities yet to come."

"Possibilities of what?"

"Your potential future. What you and this thing inside you will become." Cían pulled a pipe from inside his robes and stuffed it with a bag of dried leaves.

"I stood in a field with others. Other Mystics. But we were fighting Mystics."

He lit his pipe and breathed in a long drag. "A potential future. One you shouldn't concern yourself with."

"Shouldn't concern myself with? People were dying! And there was a person made of light."

Cían held up a hand. "The more we fret over a future we know so little about, the less control we have to change it. Be aware of the potential. When the time comes, you will know which choices will lead down that path." He stared at her for a moment longer. "However, it is interesting that some of those visions were neither yours nor mine. Seems like you and that demon are more intertwined than I previously thought."

Bastard, Asmodeus's voice echoed in Leah's head.

Leah nodded. "Why did I see visions about your grandson?"

Cían paled and shook his head. "That's none of your business."

Asmodeus laughed inside Leah's head. *Whether he wants you to see it, he needs your help.*

Leah leaned forward on her cushion. "You need our help. Your grandson's missing, isn't he? That's why I saw those visions. And I'm betting the demons we're hunting are involved."

Cían considered Leah's words. He took a drag off his pipe before he spoke. "All of that is true. My grandson, Aengus, disappeared. Over two weeks now. Demons shroud him from our visions, but every time one of us sought to find his future, it showed us Eric and this half-possessed boy."

Leah understood what Cían was asking. She also realized he wouldn't ask it outright. "You want us to find Aengus, and then you'll save Isaac?"

His blue eyes looked into hers. "If the demon that lives in your friend comes from the same demons that took my grandson, then we have a means of tracking the other demons with the blood of your friend."

"And Isaac has to still be possessed in order for the spell to work," Leah said, the pieces all falling together.

"You bring me back my grandson, and we will remove the demon from your friend."

Leah nodded and extended her hand. "Can I trust you will do everything in your power to keep him alive?"

Cían grabbed her hand and shook. "We will, but are you in a position to be making deals for your fellow Mystics?"

"You let me worry about that."

Cían leaned back and held the pipe to his lips. "Spoken like a genuine leader, Leah Ackerman."

CHAPTER 25

A MISSION OF THREE

"We're not agreeing to that," Eric said, leaning against one of the wooden columns that held up the canvas roof.

Leah looked at Sarah and Gabe, who sat silently around the circular cushions, their eyes trained on the dying embers as the first signs of morning brightened the room through the canvas walls. She'd learned Sid had left around the time Leah had to monitor Isaac. Whatever potion Cían had made her drink had lasted over an hour, and Sid hadn't returned all night.

"I know what I saw in the vision," Leah said. "They need our help as much as we need theirs."

"Who in their right mind drinks some mysterious liquid from a stranger?" Eric asked through gritted teeth, straining to keep his voice quiet. "Even if it *is* true, the risk you'd be putting us all in, and with no intel or approval from the Board. If the demons don't have our heads, the Board sure will."

Leah glared at Eric. "And yet the longer we wait, the more Isaac suffers. You came here because you wanted them to save him. Is it my fault you didn't think there'd be consequences? This is our only chance, and I'm willing to take it."

"I'm with Leah on this," Sarah said. "What other choice do we have?"

"I agree," Gabe said, his gaze locked on the embers.

Eric ran a hand through his hair and shook his head. "They can't see the future when demons are around. You're going in blind on the mere hope that the kid will be there. You screw up, and there's no saving Isaac."

Emotions hit Leah like a sledgehammer, one by one, carried through the *Yesod* bond. Anxiety, fear, and grief formed a cold sweat on her palms. Leah took in a breath, allowing his feelings to wash over her. "And if we do nothing, there's no saving him at all."

The entrance flap moved, and Sid stepped into the room. Dark bags settled underneath his reddened eyes. "They're moving him again and said I needed to come back here. They also said we'd come to some agreement?"

"She agreed to go rescue a Druid kid in exchange for Isaac's treatment," Eric said, nodding toward Leah, his arms crossed.

Sid's eyes widened. "You made a deal? Without one of us? Are you insane? If the Infinity Board finds out—"

Sarah cut him off, turning to Eric. "You brought us here, and you knew they'd probably want something in exchange for helping Isaac. So, what else did you expect?"

Eric turned away. "This is a terrible idea. Druids aren't the kind of people who make deals like this. We're going in with no idea what the dangers are while they're begging us for help. It's too dangerous."

The entrance moved again. Cloaked figures, who looked significantly less threatening in the morning light, stepped in. "The chief has summoned you. Please, come."

They walked through the small village once again.

Instead of watchful eyes, the community seemed alive and thriving around them. Nearly everyone wore long, draping clothes decorated in greens and browns. Clothes that blended well into the woods and would make it easy for them to vanish. Some whittled away at blocks of wood, carving them into totems while children sat around, copying their actions with dull blades. Others sat before large mortar and pestles, grinding dried leaves and roots together into fine powders.

Leah passed by a few generators which powered a set of stringed lights along the path and the inside of the Druids' portable homes. The scent of cooked meat and fried bacon filled Leah's nostrils as they walked past iron flattops heated by bright red embers and stoves lit by propane that cooked a breakfast fit for dozens of people.

As they continued down the path, Leah realized the community was significantly larger than she'd thought. Morning light shone on rows of canvas tents and other structures that wound beyond the main path to the larger tent, deep into the woods in both directions.

They reached a hut between two trees, set far apart from the others, and crafted from twigs bundled tightly together.

Inside, Isaac lay on a cot, his shirt removed to reveal nearly translucent alabaster skin. His breathing was ragged, and his eyes flicked back and forth as two Druids rubbed a thick, yellowed, oily substance onto him. It smelt awful, like rancid meat and garlic, with a twinge of sweetness that unsettled Leah's stomach.

Cían stood at the other end of the tent, peering over at the others who worked on Isaac. "He's stable. The salves are working well at keeping this creature at bay, encouraging him to slip into dreams." He walked around Isaac and stood in front of him. "Your friend can now rest in comfort as we use him to track down the others."

He nodded at two white-cloaked figures tending to Isaac, a short, squat man, and a tall, broad-shouldered woman, and they wiped the salve from their hands. The man rested his hands on Isaac's arms, holding him down, while the woman pulled a knife.

Sarah stepped forward. "Wait. What are you—"

Leah grabbed her arm and pulled her back. "They need his blood. Just enough to track down the demons."

The woman dragged the knife across Isaac's arm, allowing it to ooze blood. Cían held up a small glass vial to the wound, collecting it before nodding to the woman. She tended to the cut while Cían held up the vial to the light and turned the blood back and forth.

The squat man let go of Isaac and grabbed the table at the end of Isaac's bed, setting it down in front of Cían. He opened several jars, and spices filled the air.

Cían reached into one jar and pinched the contents into the vial, muttering a few words. Instantly, the thick red blood in the vial loosened up and became a bright red color. Then he pinched in another, and the mixture turned orange. Another and it changed to a dark black, which bubbled and let off an atrocious odor. Then at last, the powder he added in turned the liquid clear, and he wafted the odor to his nose. He closed his eyes and nodded.

He handed the bottle to Leah. "Do as I did and breathe slowly."

Eric groaned behind her, but she did as Cían said. Instantly, images filled her mind. She saw the encampment, then the road leading up to the camp, the highway, through the city, and lastly, an image of a warehouse burned into her mind.

Leah gave the vial to Eric, who passed it around so they could all take in the scent.

Cían nodded to the vial and said, "When you breathe this in, you'll see where the demons who caused your friend's injuries are." He handed Leah a cap to the vial. "Carry this with you in case they move." Eric cleared his throat. "They didn't even leave the city. They were right under our noses the whole time."

Cían nodded. "It would seem so. Bring back my grandson, and we will save your Mystic."

Eric stepped forward. "The Infinity Board needs to know about this. They need to approve it. If we go in there, we risk the Board coming down on our heads."

Cían tutted his tongue. "We have made a bargain, Mizrahi."

"Yes, you have. With someone who doesn't have the authority to speak for the Infinity Board, or this group."

Cían sighed. "I'd hoped you'd say something different."

In an instant, the two white-cloaked figures raised their palms to Eric and Sid, blowing an orange powder into their faces. They both crumpled to the ground in an instant.

Energy filled the room as the three standing Mystics filled their bodies with *Malchut*.

Cían held up both his hands and focused on Leah. "It was always a probability that your Knight and Bishop would not agree to the terms of your bargain. Once Eric said that you do not speak for the Board, then all other possibilities would lead to delay or death. Two things neither of us have time for."

Fire burst into Sarah's hand as she glared. "You can't know that. He hadn't even decided yet."

Leah squeezed Sarah's shoulder. "Sarah, wait. Hear him out."

Sarah snuffed out her flames and crossed her arms.

Cían turned his gaze to Sarah. "He'd decided in his mind. Anything else would have been stalling for time while he planned a new bargain, one that would have killed at least three of you. This is the best way to sneak in and out."

Gabe shook his head. "We're just Pawns. How are we supposed to rescue your grandson? You took away the best chance we had."

Leah squeezed the vial in her hands. "We don't have time to argue. We know where we need to go. I trust them to have made the best choice for us." Her eyes stayed on Gabe for a moment before turning to the exit.

They stopped for gas after reaching the edge of the city, using cash Cían gave them before they'd left.

Sarah stared down at her half-eaten protein bar she'd bought and said, "Why didn't we just steal the potion?"

"What?" Leah asked, as she sped away from the gas station.

"The potion. The one that would save Isaac. We could have just taken it from them. I bet we could have fought them off."

Gabe scoffed. "Fight off a group of nomadic warriors capable of predicting your moves? They'd have seen you stealing the vial before you even decided."

"Nomadic warriors? Where'd you hear that from?" Sarah asked.

"Sid. His lessons with Isaac and I are kind of intense. I also know that simply having the potion wouldn't work. It has to be administered by a Druid, I think."

"Why?" Sarah asked.

"The stuff in it only works if the person using it has some sort of connection or understanding. It was hard to follow when Sid started mentioning 'quantum mechanics on a macro scale' but basically, they might not work unless you are a trained Druid."

"Good thing we didn't try the hard way then," Leah said, focusing on the road.

They drove in silence until they passed the exit that would have taken them back to the orphanage. Gabe cleared his throat and said, "That was weird, right? Back there, at the orphanage. I mean, that nurse was clearly possessed, but no one saw her with *Tiferet*. Had any of us actually seen her, maybe we wouldn't be in this mess. But I checked that room with the bookcase at least twice."

Sarah leaned back in the passenger seat and looked up at the roof. "Who knows? She was in a secret room. For all we know, there's some magic spell that can conceal them or something. It's not like we know every ritual or spell that works."

Gabe shifted in his seat and shook his head. "Maybe, but I haven't heard of anything that can do that. You'd think the Infinity Board would know about it."

Leah squeezed the steering wheel. "That room was different. The ritual that took place. It was strange. An abomination." She felt goosebumps going down her back as she recalled Asmodeus's words.

"Maybe I can go through some of Sid's books when we're back at the academy. He seems to have some of the most detailed things there are about demons," Gabe said.

Sarah held up her fists and clenched them until her knuckles cracked. "And then we'll give them hell. They won't stand a chance."

Leah smirked, but when she looked in the rearview mirror, her gaze met Gabe's sullen face. "But how are we even going to sneak in? Without Eric and Sid, this is suicide."

Sneak in. Those words hit Leah, and she knew exactly what the Druids wanted her to do. "Sneak in. Ugh. I'm an idiot." She slammed her hand on the wheel.

"What?" Sarah asked.

"I can sneak in. I know how to go unnoticed."

"Unnoticed? What, like the nurse?" Gabe asked.

"Exactly like that."

"Leah, are you sure that's a good idea?" Sarah asked.

Leah nodded. "I know a way. As long as it works this time."

Asmodeus sighed in her ear. *Perhaps consuming a little corruption will speed up my healing.*

"What are you talking about? As long as *what* works?" Gabe asked, eying Sarah and Leah.

Sarah looked over at Leah. "I don't think you should tell—"

Leah cut her off. "I can make myself invisible. I used it a few times to sneak out of the academy back when we were Black Pawns. Only problem is . . . it comes from the Tree of Death."

Gabe shook his head. "Absolutely not. We'll find a different way in. Are you serious right now? You are *not* using the Tree of Death."

Leah turned off the highway, letting the fumes of the potion guide them to their destination. She sighed. "That is probably why Cían would send us without Eric or Sid. It has to be. What else could get us in? Could get *me* in? I can grab Cían's grandson and get out undetected."

Gabe cradled his head in his hands. "This is insane. Neither of them know? Not even Eric? Why? How?"

"It's complicated, okay? Just, please, trust me on this." Leah met his eyes in the rearview.

Sarah looked back at Gabe and lightly punched his leg. "Look man, I'm not a fan of it either, but it makes sense. She used it a handful of times, even on me, and nothing happened."

"Nothing's happened *yet*," Gabe said.

Sarah looked at him, her eyes welling up. "Look, this could be our best shot to save Isaac. It might be our only shot. Clearly, the Druids knew something like this would work, so I side with Leah on this. We can get the whole lecture on it after."

Gabe crossed his arms and remained quiet until the van came to a stop. They were in a neighborhood filled with abandoned houses. Had it been night, it would have been an eerie sight to see so many boarded-up windows. In broad daylight, it was sadder than anything.

Leah unbuckled her seatbelt and looked back at Gabe. "You take the wheel. Sarah, I'll have you on comms."

Sarah tapped her earpiece and held it down. Leah heard her friend's voice in her ear. "Ready."

Gabe reached over and grabbed Leah's hand and squeezed. "Just be careful, okay?"

"I will," Leah said.

CHAPTER 26

THAGIRION

Leah stepped out of the van and pulled the small vial from her coat. She uncorked the top and breathed in. Visions filled her mind, one of which provided an overlay over the empty street another a few blocks down.

"Looks like it's just up ahead," Leah said. "Keep the car back here for now until I give the all clear."

"Copy that," the voice in her ear said.

As Leah continued down the street, Asmodeus spoke in her mind. *Not that you care much for my opinion, but I think your Druid friends are setting you up to be killed.*

"Great timing," Leah whispered. "Don't you think it's a little late for that?"

You were preoccupied with the others. I assumed talking to yourself was not something you were interested in.

"Well, we're already in the thick of it, and I'm saving Isaac, no matter what."

Leah heard an audible sigh coming from inside her mind. *I know, but I still wished to express my concern. That and there is something you should know about Thagirion.*

Leah stopped at the intersection and took another smell of the vial. "Really great timing. What is it?"

It moves your body into a space between the physical and the Astral Realm. You aren't invisible; you're somewhere else. But things in the Astral can see you. When fresh meat shows up on that side, it attracts demons and other things you'd rather not know about.

Memories of the ghost following her in the library and chasing after her and her friends flashed through her mind. Razor-sharp teeth, and a mouth stretched unnaturally far, reaching into the back of Sid's truck before Leah let go of *Thagirion.* "So what? I can't use it then?"

Asmodeus stayed quiet for a long moment while Leah kept walking down the empty street. Then his voice rang in her ears again. *The possessed ones won't see if you use Thagirion. You'd only have to worry if they have demons patrolling the Astral Realm. It would be like a beacon to them, so you'd have to get in and out quickly. Do you understand?*

Leah continued down the winding streets, periodically stopping to smell from the vial and match the visions to the houses in front of her. "Legion could be here. Do you think he'd see me?"

He won't be here. This is too beneath him, Asmodeus said.

"How are you so certain?"

A puppet master does not sleep with the puppets. Besides, this . . . babysitting . . . has its risks, and he wouldn't want to be around if the Infinity Board caught wind. Not yet at least.

Leah let out a breath she didn't know she was holding. At least she didn't have to deal with Legion just yet. "You seem to know him well . . ."

Our paths crossed many times, and it didn't end well for me.

She wanted to know more, but as she turned down the next road, the homes gave way to an empty lot and a warehouse that matched the image from the vial.

Leah ducked behind a set of overgrown shrubs in front of a blue home with peeling paint. Ahead, she could see a barbed wire fence that led up to a gated entrance in the middle of the road. She held her hand up to her ear. "In position. You should be able to drive up two blocks and park without them seeing you."

"Copy," Sarah replied. "Room for us to converge on your point?"

Leah looked up and down the street. "Affirmative. There are some shrubs that should give us a vantage point and a direct line straight to the van. I'll hold position."

Sarah and Gabe showed up five minutes later and looked out at the warehouse.

"I need to get closer for *Tiferet* to pick up anything," Leah said.

Gabe nodded and was about to stand up when Sarah held his arm. "I can do it from here."

Before either of them could speak, Leah felt the familiar twinge of energy in the air, and Sarah's eyes flared with golden light. A few minutes later, Sarah spoke. "Wow, okay. Glad we stayed back. I'm counting at least twenty. Two guarding the front, two in the back, four patrolling the roof, maybe five inside, and at least six patrolling the perimeter."

Gabe looked in the van's direction, sighed, then turned back. "Can you keep an eye on them a little longer, see if there are any openings for Leah to get in? I'll carry you back to the car if your vision goes."

Sarah nodded. "I don't see any open windows Leah could reach."

"I think I could follow behind one of them and get in," Leah said.

Gabe bit his lip. "You think you can stay concealed doing that?"

"Yes. Once it's on, it doesn't take much to maintain.

When I get inside, I'll make contact with Aengus, shroud him, and retrace my steps."

"And you can't shroud one of us to go with you? We could help," Gabe said.

Asmodeus spoke in Leah's head. *That would attract even more attention.*

Leah shook her head. "No, I need you as my getaway, and Sarah needs to recoup her sight."

Minutes passed, and Leah and Gabe crouched in silence while Sarah continued to scan.

Gabe rested a hand on Leah's knee and looked up at her. "I just want you to be safe. If you get into any trouble, I'll drive that van through that gate and get you out, okay?"

Leah grabbed his hand and smiled. "I might just ask you to so I can see you try."

Gabe leaned in and kissed her. "I'm serious. If things take a turn, let me help."

Sarah blinked a few times and waved her arms until Leah caught her hand. Sarah's eyes darted around; the golden hue was gone. "Well, I can't see now." She rubbed her eyes. "Seems like someone from outside switches places with someone inside about every fifteen minutes. That should give you enough time to get into position and get in undetected."

Leah checked her gun once more. "Okay, I'll conceal, then squeeze in through the gate. Keep radio chatter to emergencies only from now on. Gabe, just be ready to tear out of here."

Sarah gripped Leah's shoulder. "Just come back in one piece. If you wind up dead, I hope you know I'm gonna revive you somehow just so I can kill you again for going through with this plan."

Leah rested a hand on Sarah's hand, a small smile on her lips. "Noted."

She turned to Gabe, and he raised his eyebrows. "Same goes for me."

Leah planted a kiss on Gabe's lips, staying for a moment, and pulled away. "Well, glad to know you two have a backup plan."

Before they said another word, Leah closed her eyes focused on the energy emanating from her arm. A sensation of cold, thick gel oozed over her body, covering her left arm before creeping over the rest of her. Sounds around her dulled and faded into silence.

Mmm. I already taste the corruption.

She opened her eyes, and Gabe and Sarah stood in front of her, partially faded from her vision. Everything else changed. The blue-flecked house behind her was completely leveled, and the ground beneath her was covered in dried yellow grass. She looked down at her arm, black markings tattooed from the demon mark.

She clenched her fist and whispered, "Let's do this."

Leah approached the gate and spotted an opening between it and the fence. She squeezed through and crouched down low.

She took her time with gun in hand as she crossed the parking lot, keeping her distance from the guards so they wouldn't hear her footsteps. No one reacted, not even a pause from their circular walk along the perimeter.

When she was five yards from the building, she slowed, carefully stepping past a guard posted near the door's entrance. She leaned against the building inches from the door, and as she did so, the guard turned and looked right at her.

Leah held her breath, her finger resting on the trigger of her gun. She hadn't contemplated what she'd have to do if they caught her. Didn't have time to consider if she'd really have to pull the trigger.

The guard's eyes unfocused and trailed along the wall left and right before looking back out at the parking lot. She let out a slow breath and pressed against the wall and waited.

An old man wearing a canary yellow polo and golf shorts walked up past the guard and to the door next to Leah. She could smell his disgusting breath, the breath of a man who had skipped brushing his teeth for several days, as he entered the code on the door.

It beeped a few times, and he pulled it open. She didn't have time to pause, as she held her breath and used the sound of the door opening to her advantage, slipping in right in front of the man.

He stepped in a second later, and Leah had to maneuver out of his way, pressing herself up against the inside wall.

They stood inside an old front office, complete with broken and dusted-over tabled and ceiling panels. She followed the old man down the hall, turning left, then right, until he reached the doors to the main warehouse.

Following him through the doors, a pungent smell of unclean clothes and bodies hit her.

Then she saw them.

Nearly a hundred kids huddled together in little sleeping bags with the five guards circling them. From what she saw, none of them looked as emaciated as the child back at that orphanage.

The old man swapped positions with another guard, who then proceeded out the doors.

Even though the shroud of *Thagirion* masked most sounds, Leah knew how quiet it was in the room. No talking, whimpers, or sniffles came from the kids, and the guards moved like silent robots.

You need to move quickly, Asmodeus said.

Leah approached the children and knelt beside one of

them. In the dim light, she made out a thin brown girl, only six or seven, lying completely still, her eyes open and staring up at the ceiling.

Before she could ask the question on her mind, Asmodeus answered. *I don't see any possession, but they're all in a trance. Powerful demons can do that.*

Leah gritted her teeth. She imagined how it must feel, trapped in their own bodies, stuck staring up at a ceiling. Afraid. Taken from their families.

The little girl's eyes flitted and landed on Leah. They stared at each other for a moment, no emotion on the little girl's face, her eyes unblinking.

Leah's stomach tied itself in knots. The thought of these children trapped here filled her with a rage that pushed on the edge of her skin. She felt like she was going to explode. She felt the *Malchut* inside her building.

Snap out of it, Asmodeus hissed in her ear. *Get the child and get out. If you try anything else, we'll both die.*

Leah let out a slow breath and backed away, noting that the girl's eyes followed her as she started around the circle of children.

Halfway through, she spotted him—red hair and freckles, with green eyes staring lifelessly up toward the ceiling. She tiptoed around several kids gently so she didn't accidentally end up stepping on one of them.

Leah stopped beside him, three kids deep in the circle of children, and knelt. She focused on the energy that shrouded her, the cool thick gel, and reached out and grabbed onto Aengus's shoulder. The invisible substance flowed from her hand and started its way across his body.

The moment the energy covered his eyes, he blinked several times and looked right at her. He smiled as tears formed in his eyes.

Leah had him. Relief washed over her. She had him. All

she had to do was bring him back, and the Druids would
save Isaac.

But then she jumped as the other children screamed.

CHAPTER 27
TEAMWORK

The screams coming from the children bore through Leah's skull, leaving behind a high-pitched ring as she attempted to cover her ears while holding on to Aengus.

She pulled him up to his feet, wrapping her arm around him and dragging him toward the exit. They were still invisible, and the possessed adults all turned to face the children, their eyes unable to locate their invisible target as they let out strange clicks and hisses.

They had only one row of sleeping bags to pass before they'd break free from the screaming children. One more step and they would be in the clear. But Leah's foot caught on one of the sleeping bags, and she tumbled forward, slamming her knee on the hard concrete floor.

The child she had tripped over leaped on top of her, screaming in her face. Others joined in immediately after, pinning her and Aengus down as they clawed and scratched at her. Through the gaps between children, she saw the adults closing in, their fingers outstretched like claws.

No, not like this, she thought.

Energy blossomed inside of her, filling every crevice with light and pressing up against her skin. She squeezed onto Aengus as she let out a burst of *Malchut*, sending the kids flying back and tumbling into the adults. With *Thagirion* still shrouding them, she pulled Aengus and started toward the exit, but he stopped her. She looked back, half expecting him to scream too, but his wide eyes looked to the others, his mouth trying to work. "What about—"

Leah pulled on his arm. "Not yet. We will. Later."

That answer seemed to be enough, and she dragged him along toward the door. Ice shivered down her spine, and she let in a gasp as energy flooded into her. Before she could even think, her arm aimed at the door and blasted a wave of energy that tore it from its hinges.

The guard standing out front now lay motionless under the metal door as they passed.

Demons screamed behind her, and as Leah stepped onto the asphalt parking lot, she knew they'd come out the door in search of her. The others outside flocked toward their screaming brethren, closing in on Leah. Demons on the other side of the building came racing around with inhuman speed, and in the blink of an eye, dozens of demons surrounded her, converging on her point. They still couldn't see her, but she had nowhere to go.

Asmodeus groaned and whispered in her ear. *I am well enough now. Let me take over.*

She didn't have time to argue with him. In an instant, it was as if something untied invisible ropes around Leah, and whatever claim she had of her body vanished. The markings on her left arm grew darker and darker until it engulfed her arm in a solid black shadow, and her fingers had elongated into sharpened claws.

Whispers crept in and surrounded her, growing louder

and louder, drowning out all other sounds. Then black smoke pooled around her arm. Her fist closed, and the smoke was sucked into her arm. Wind blew through her hair, and she struggled to breathe, as if her arm had become a vacuum.

All the demons stumbled forward, pulled by the sudden force of *Nehemoth, Malchut's* opposite. It kept pulling, dragging in energy around Leah and packing more and more into her arm. She felt the building of energy, felt it filling her whole body unnaturally, screaming to be let back out.

Use Malchut, Asmodeus said.

She regained sensation, wrapped both arms around Aengus, and released the energy.

It tore out of her, cutting into the asphalt as it rammed into the demons and sent them all flying back with a massive concussive force.

Now . . . His voice became a distant echo, mixed in among the whispers, and Leah heard Asmodeus say, *Run!*

Leah grabbed on tight to Aengus's hand and rushed past demons who lay dazed, scraped, and bruised. The cold gel of *Thagirion* melted away with each step she took, and color and life came back to her senses.

She pushed through the gates and turned down the street to the van. She pressed down on her earbud. "Sarah, I have Aengus. We're on your six."

"Copy," Sarah said. The van's engine rumbled to life a moment later.

Leah opened the back doors and helped Aengus in before getting in and slamming the doors behind her. "Go! Go! Go!"

Tires squealed as Gabe rammed his foot on the gas and tore out of there, leaving behind the abandoned homes and merging onto the highway.

Once the adrenaline had settled, and she was certain no

one had followed, Leah collapsed in her seat. Every muscle in her body ached, and she looked over her left arm, noting a few shallow cuts on her skin that she suspected came from whatever Asmodeus did.

Aengus sat next to her, his eyes staring forward, tears on his cheeks.

She'd saved him; that's what mattered. That's all she thought about as she drifted out of consciousness.

Leah sat in a chair in front of a marble table in the middle of a vast black ocean, staring down at a hand that flickered between an inhuman black claw and her own.

"We make a good team, you and I," Asmodeus said from across the white table, looking over his own hand, which had healed completely from the last time she saw it. He looked healthier too. More solid, with even a little color in his cheeks as opposed to his usual form. His eyes were back to their pitch black. However, a tiny pinprick of light stayed, like a bright star in a void of nothing.

Leah shook her left hand until it stopped flickering, only showing its normal human form. "That was close. *Too* close."

"And yet it could have been worse. Creatures from the Astral can be even more unpredictable."

Images of her arm, skin torn from whatever Asmodeus had done, flashed in her mind. "Well, I didn't like it."

"Like what?"

"You. Taking over." Her arm flickered once again into a blackened claw. "Doing this to me and nearly tearing me apart."

Asmodeus smirked and leaned back in his chair. "Yet

the power, the thrill. You can't tell me you didn't enjoy at least some of it."

She slammed her blackened fist onto the table, cracking the marble countertop. Her heart pounded fast, and her arm flickered back into her own. "I keep using the Tree of Death. The whispers, they were everywhere. Am I . . . am I losing it? Am I corrupted?"

"No. You've allowed me to call on the Tree of Death, not you. I take the corruption, feed off it, and you don't suffer from the ill effects. But even I have my limits. If you call too much of it before I can take on the corruption, that may be a different story. I wouldn't want you dying before you save your friends."

Leah tilted her head. "Since when do you care about saving others?"

"I care about keeping you intact. If you die now, I die. Simple as that."

Leah shook her head. "You helped me save Isaac back at the orphanage. If you only cared about me, you'd have blasted me out of that room without him."

The demon eyed Leah, unblinking, before saying, "Your sanity is important. If that gets jeopardized because one of your friends died, then I—"

"I don't believe you!" Leah shouted. "Stop deflecting and just admit it."

Asmodeus didn't speak. Instead, he stood and walked to the edge of the white-walled room.

"Hey, I'm talking to you!" Leah shouted.

Asmodeus turned, his face smooth as he pointed a long bony finger at her arm. It flickered back into a clawed arm for a moment. "You might want to get a hold of that. Assuming you still want to push me away." His voice changed, sounding just like Sarah's as he said, "We're almost there."

Leah furrowed her brows. "What?"

Sarah's voice pulled her out of the black ocean and back into reality. "I said we're almost there. Get up."

Leah stretched her arms and looked out at the morning sun, partially blocked by the forest canopy. "How far out are we?"

Gabe looked back into the rearview mirror. "Five minutes, tops. Just took the last turn onto the gravel road. Are you up to speak to the chief?"

"Yeah. Yeah, I just need to shake off this sleep." Leah wiped her eyes.

Cloaked figures appeared out of the trees, and Gabe had to slam on the brakes to miss them. He huffed as he killed the engine and stepped out.

Leah looked over at Aengus, who was in the same position he had been in when he got in the car, eyes trained forward, reddened from tears.

"You're home now," Leah said. "You're safe."

Aengus didn't respond. Leah unbuckled him and helped him out of the car, following the cloaked figures with Sarah and Gabe walking behind them.

As they raced down the main dirt path, all the Druids stopped what they were doing to stare. They entered the large tent to find Cían sitting around the fire, surrounded by cloaked figures on either side.

Leah led Aengus closer and said, "We brought your grandson back. Now, please, fulfill your side of the bargain."

The old man nodded to two white cloaks, the same two who'd tended to Isaac. They came to Aengus's side and checked him over. They pulled on him to bring him closer to Cían, but Leah held onto him. "No. Not until you fulfill your end of the bargain."

Cían looked at the white-cloaked figures, and one of them spoke in hushed whispers. "He still has the demon's trance on him, but we should be able to free him from that in no time."

Cían looked at Leah and smiled. "You have done a great service to me and my people. Our word is our honor."

He nodded to the doors behind them, and more cloaked figures stepped through, carrying Isaac on a stretcher. They laid him in front of the fire and backed away. Cían stood, pulling out a small glass bottle with a clear liquid inside. "This has the potential to go sideways, and this demon may be more resistant than we're prepared for. Your friend has been quite resilient, though. He should make it through this."

He poured the liquid into Isaac's mouth.

Isaac convulsed.

With each shake of his body, a thrum of energy rippled through the air, resonating in Leah's chest. The fire beside him rose higher, and heat bellowed out from the center of the room.

Cían let out a low, guttural tone as he stood and held out his hands. Other Druids joined in around him, clasping hands and letting out a harmonic tone as the thrums of energy emanated off Isaac.

Isaac's back arched, and he let out a wretched scream that pierced through Leah's ears. She winced. Then color came back to her friend's face, and the black lines on his flesh receded to three black gouges on his stomach, converging into a thin line that traveled up his neck and onto the side of his face. He slowly lowered back down onto the stretcher, and he let in deep, slow breaths as his head slumped to the side.

Cían let go of the others and stepped around Isaac, standing in front of Leah. "He will need rest, but he is safe from death for now. Those marks won't fade, and they could cause a disruption around his future. One of the side effects of dealing with demons, I'm afraid."

He stepped aside and rested a hand on Aengus as Leah and her friends rushed to Isaac's side. His once cold and clammy skin was now warm, and any sign of pain was washed free from his face. Sarah brushed away a tear while she squeezed his hand. Leah stood next to Gabe, running a finger along the mark on Isaac's cheek. A tingle, like static electricity, traveled up her arm.

"May we speak one last time, Leah? Before your Knight and Bishop wake."

Gabe grabbed Leah's hand and hissed. "Don't. For all you know, he'll just want another bargain. We got what we came for."

Sarah caught Leah's gaze and nodded. "Let's just go."

Leah bit her lip and looked at Cían. She then turned back to her friends. "Take Isaac back to the van. Eric and Sid will want to get out of here the moment they get up. I'll be there soon."

Gabe huffed but didn't argue. Both he and Sarah picked up the stretcher and carried Isaac out without speaking another word.

Cían watched them leave. "We are leaving as well. Today. We've already overstayed our visit, and there are plenty of other forests that could use us."

"Why are you telling me this?"

"Our paths will not cross for a long time. The company you surround yourself with shrouds your life in more ways than one, but one thing I am certain of is that you will need this."

He handed Leah a small, corked bottle. Inside was thick green liquid, and as Leah turned it over, she felt an icy shiver run through her fingers.

"What is it?" she asked.

"One of our strongest potions, and the purest essence of mandrake you'll ever find. It will tear out any being not of this world from a body of flesh and bone."

"I . . ."

Cían closed his hand around hers and gripped the bottle tight. "I'm not telling you to use it. And I'm not telling you to *not* use it. This is a choice you must make on your own, and one I trust you will know to make when the time comes. Remember what your friend Gabriel said to you? A potion from us only works if you believe it will. The path ahead will test you in more ways than one. Be steadfast and know yourself." He let go of her hand and turned on his heel.

Leah looked down at the potion, her jaw fighting against her to work. "Wait. How do you know I have what it takes? How do you know I'll make the right choice?"

The old man turned and stared into her eyes. "For the things I cannot see, I must have faith."

CHAPTER 28
LIES & THREATS

"Not a word until I speak with Leah. Alone. Understood?" Eric's voice hovered in the van for a moment as Sid turned into the gated entrance of the academy.

Sid glanced in the rearview mirror, his eyes locking with Gabe's for a moment. Gabe then turned around in his seat and looked at Isaac, checking his vitals. "He's still not awake, but he's stable."

Sid nodded and drew in a sharp breath. "Not a word."

They rounded the last bend in the driveway, and Sarah looked out her window and spotted a familiar face standing on the steps to the academy. "Wait, is that Queen Nielsen?"

Leah recognized her instantly. She wore a black pantsuit that hugged her slim body and drew Leah's eyes up to her short blond hair styled in a quaff. On her left, Constance hid her exhaustion behind a fake smile and stood with a rigid posture to match her wool white and black dress. Grace stood on Helen's other side, in a white pantsuit similar to Helen's, her hands folded in front of her. None of the other Pawns were with them. Instead, a small group of armed security stood behind them.

Sid parked the van in front the steps and shut off the engine.

Once they stepped out, the Queen wasted no time. "Good evening. Please, let us take our injured Pawn to the infirmary at once and assess his wounds."

She nodded, and the guards encircled Sid and Gabe as they pulled Isaac out from the back of the van and carried him up the steps and into the infirmary.

The group moved inside, and the guards placed him on the nearest bed and stepped back while Helen and Constance took to either side of Isaac. They held their hands above him and shut their eyes.

A chilly breeze emanated from them, swirling around Leah's head and filling her mind with thoughts of sleep and comfort. Had it gone on any longer, Leah was certain she'd collapse where she stood.

Instead, the breeze stopped, and Helen said, "He's stable. No signs of corruption or possession detected. Only a scar that will mark his bravery."

Constance nodded and looked at Eric. "Looks like your gamble paid off."

Helen waved off the guards and waited until they left to look over the team that brought Isaac back. "Grace tells me he was on the brink of death. Your quick actions kept a young Mystic alive, and for that you should be immensely proud, as am I. I want to tell you about what comes next, but you all deserve a much-needed rest, I'm sure. We'll convene tomorrow."

Before Helen had a chance to order them off, Sarah looked around the infirmary and asked, "What about the kid? How's he doing?"

Helen looked at the other occupied bed down near the window. The boy lay there, hooked up to an IV and a tiny monitor.

Constance cleared her throat. "He hasn't woken up yet. We can't detect anything wrong with him, but he's in a deep sleep that we can't pull him out of. For now, we're monitoring him and hoping he wakes soon."

Helen smiled and gestured for them to exit the infirmary. "You're all dismissed. Please, rest up."

As they entered the halls, Eric pulled Leah away from the others and into the library. "We're having our talk. Now."

Eric flipped on the lights and led Leah to a corner of the room overlooking the back fields. The sun had set, and the faint purple light was fading fast into darkness. "How about we start with what you and Cían talked about?"

Leah stared at the dark circles under Eric's eyes before speaking. "He gave me tea, and we looked into my past and possible future."

"Why? Why'd he pick you out of all of us? Did he say?"

Leah felt a twinge in her left arm, but she tried her best not to react. Obviously, he'd picked her because of Asmodeus. She bit her lip. "Something about my future had him worried, I guess. It was all fractured. I could barely understand any of it."

Eric grunted. "And knocking Sid and I out, what was the point of that?"

"Cían said you'd both get in the way. He needed his grandson back and if you two came along, it was probable that one or three of us were going to die." Her heart was beating in her chest as she focused on the stacks behind him. There it was, the creature that had followed them on Sid's truck, the young boy peeking from the stacks. However, as soon as he caught her eye, he vanished.

"That was really stupid. You three are lucky you're even alive. You could have died, or worse, been possessed. Did you want that? They'd have used you too, forced you to come back and kill us, and you'd be stuck watching it all happen with no control of your own body."

Leah's breath caught in her throat. "I'm ... I'm sorry."

Eric shook his head and balled his fists. "Stop being sorry and just trust me for once!"

Leah felt pain ripple through her bond. He'd spoken these words before, to someone else, and it hurt for him to say them again. Leah never knew Jade, nor wanted to pry into Eric's past, but she suspected Jade had been a lot like her, and all Eric wanted was to be trusted.

"I promise, if I'd done something wrong, I'd tell you," Leah said. "Cían knocked you two out before I knew what he was going to do. When he told me the odds, I believed him. I was focused on saving Isaac, no matter what."

Eric wrapped an arm around Leah and held her tight. Grief intermixed with pain through the *Yesod* bond, and Leah returned his embrace, hoping to ease even a fraction of what he felt.

When he finally spoke, Eric said, "I'm just glad that you're okay. If you wound up dead. If you—"

The doors to the library opened. Eric let go of Leah, and with it, the feelings in the *Yesod* bond retreated. Leah knew he'd cut himself off again, bottled up his feelings in a poor attempt to stay stoic.

Nykima rounded the corner, her eyes on Eric. "Queen Nielsen wants to have a word."

Eric looked back toward Leah. "Go get some rest, okay?"

Leah watched as Eric followed Nykima out of the library. She took in the silence, finally back at the academy. Finally safe.

She started toward the exit when Gabe popped out from behind the stacks. "So, what? He doesn't know and you're just not going to tell him?"

Leah froze. "Were you here the whole time?"

Gabe nodded. "I followed you in. Wanted to make sure Eric wouldn't make any rash decisions."

She glared at him. "That wasn't a conversation for you to hear."

"I know. But I care about you. I worry about you. And you keep putting yourself in dangerous situations without a care for who it hurts."

Leah spotted the tears forming in his eyes, but she stood her ground as anger bubbled up inside her. "Would you rather Isaac be dead right now? You don't know anything, Gabe. I'm done."

"Done?"

Leah realized she hit a nerve she hadn't meant to and quickly fumbled over her words. "With this conversation, you idiot. Not us . . . or whatever this is."

Gabe slowly nodded and looked at the floor. His eyes flicked up to her arm. "I saw your arm, you know."

A chill ran down her neck. "My arm?"

"We stayed back in the bushes. Waited there in case you needed backup. I saw those demons closing in on something in the parking lot. I knew it was you, and I wanted to come in and help, but Sarah stopped me. You pushed them all back in one hit stronger than anything I'd seen. I used *Tiferet*, just to get a better look. That's when I saw it. Your arm was black, clawed. It wasn't . . . human."

Leah opened and closed her hand, taking a step back. "I don't know what you're talking about."

Gabe approached her and grabbed her arm. "Stop lying. Please. Just stop." Tears rolled down his cheeks, and he held his lips to her hands. "Don't make the same mistake I did. People died. I know you think you have it under control, but you don't. Trust me. Please."

Leah pulled away, shaking her head. "I . . . I can't"

"You have to. Tell them everything. How you use the Tree of Death, and whatever that claw is. Please. For us."

Asmodeus whispered in her ear, *And what would they do to the Pawn who kept a demon hidden from them?*

"I can't," Leah repeated.

Gabe stepped back. "Then I don't know if I can do this 'us' thing anymore. If you care about me at all, you'll tell them."

"Gabe don't do that. Don't make me—"

"Noon, tomorrow. You have until then to decide. If you don't tell them, I will." He turned and stomped out of the library, leaving Leah alone with her thoughts.

Leah watched the doors close behind Gabe. She clenched her fists and squeezed her eyes shut. He didn't understand. He couldn't understand.

She stomped toward the door, her next steps reeling through her mind.

"Wait," a whisper called behind her.

Leah stopped, her hand shaking on the door handle. She turned, peering out into the empty library.

A form materialized in front of her. A young boy, pale, with wisps of smoke curling off him. It was the same boy she'd seen so many times before, the same boy that could turn into a monster any second.

"I don't like it," he said.

Leah frowned, her frustration with Gabe still bubbling up to the surface. "I don't have time for this. What don't you like?"

The boy pointed past her, his eyes wide. "That child doesn't belong here."

Leah looked behind her at the closed library door. Beyond that was the infirmary.

She eyed the ghostly boy, and his head twitched, his innocent face contorting and elongating while razor-sharp teeth and white eyes stared at her. "It's not welcome," he hissed.

Cold sweat formed on the back of her neck, but she stood firm, eyes locked on the ghost.

"Do you mean the child we brought back? Why? Why doesn't he belong?"

"He's broken. And he smells of death. Destroy him now, before his death spreads."

Leah glared at the boy. "We're going to do everything we can to save him. If you do anything to hurt him . . ."

The ghost's face contorted back into a boy, and he looked down at his feet. "He doesn't belong here."

Leah raised a finger at the boy, growing more frustrated. "I don't know what your deal is, but I've had enough. You do anything to that child, and I'll tell everyone about you!"

His form shifted again, and he stretched tall above her, ghostly saliva dripping from his maw.

Leah remained, feet planted on the ground. "You want to stay here, right?"

The ghost was a boy again, backing up, phasing into the stacks.

Leah stomped her foot. "Wait, I'm not done with you!"

CHAPTER 29

INNER FEARS

Leah walked into the third-floor common room and slammed the door behind her. Sarah, wrapped in nothing but a towel, paused en route to her room to stare at Leah. "What's wrong?"

Leah started toward her bedroom, her fists opening and closing. "Boys are so stupid."

Sarah followed her and smirked. "Tell me something I don't know. But if it makes you feel any better, girls are just as bad. Only in a different way."

Leah moved in close to Sarah and raised her left arm. "Gabe knows."

Sarah's eyes widened, and she ushered Leah into her room, closing the door behind her. "Wait. How?"

"The parking lot. They surrounded us. I let Asmodeus help, and Gabe saw it." Leah slumped onto Sarah's second bed, Leah's old bed when the academy was still a school, and crossed her arms.

Her heart pounded in her chest, and all she could think of was the look on Eric's face when he found out. She'd be kicked out of the academy, and he'd be without a Pawn again.

She looked out the window, contemplating fleeing, when Sarah kicked at her leg. "Hey, get up. We're going for a walk."

Leah pulled herself out of her daze and looked at Sarah, who'd dressed in sweatpants, a white T-shirt, and white sneakers. "Why?"

Sarah looked around. "Thin walls. And you need air, trust me."

Night had already settled on the academy, casting the stairs and halls into darkness. They descended to the first floor. A creak sounded behind them, and Leah jumped, slowly turning.

Joanna tiptoed down the steps, brushing past Leah and Sarah before turning around and smiling.

"What are you doing?" Sarah asked.

Joanna slipped her hands into her pockets and grinned, backing up to the front doors. "I could ask you two the same."

She creaked open the doors and slipped out without another word.

Sarah turned to Leah and whispered, "I think she's dating a guard now. I overheard her talking about some new boy toy, and none of the Pawns knew who she was talking about."

Leah shrugged. "Whatever makes her happy, I guess."

They turned and stepped out into the night, taking in the clear star-filled sky.

Sarah took a deep breath and stretched. "I don't know about you, but I already feel better."

Leah copied Sarah, stretching and looking toward the horizon at the rising half-moon. "Wow, yeah, all my panic is just completely gone."

Sarah laughed. "Okay. Fine, don't enjoy it. But why don't you tell me what's going on?"

"Gabe gave me an ultimatum. He said I have to either tell Eric everything or he's going to. He gave me by noon tomorrow to make a decision. Even if I pretend, Gabe has enough to make Eric suspicious. Enough that it would only be a matter of time before they found out."

Sarah nodded. "He cares about you."

"If he did, then he'd drop it."

Sarah crossed her arms. "I drop it because I'm willing to trust that you have it under control. He can't. Not with what happened to him. That, and he likes you. *Really* likes you."

"Yeah, but what's happening to me is different. Asmodeus didn't possess me. He broke free from Legion's command and almost died from it. The part of him that lived on is different, and it wants to end Legion just as much as I do."

"Hold up. You weren't too keen on siding with the demon before. What's changed now?"

Leah shrugged. "I don't know. He's saved me and helped me with Isaac too. I don't know if it's some sort of con, but it doesn't feel that way. Maybe something inside me is hoping that whatever piece of him that lived wasn't the part that wanted to kill my mom."

Sarah grabbed on to Leah's shoulder. "Yeah, but you can't forgive and forget. This is Asmodeus, the demon who led a war that attacked and killed hundreds of Mystics. The monster that killed your mom and possessed your dad. He's not some good savior. Never will be. No amount of good can clear the evils he's done."

And what of the evils she's done? No hand stays clean for long, Asmodeus hissed in Leah's ear.

Leah shrugged off Sarah and said, "If he's just evil, then why would he even care to save Isaac? He helped me. He cared. When I needed help, he pulled Isaac out of that room before that thing could fully possess him."

"He's a demon. All they want is to sit inside you and eat away at your soul until you die. Whatever he's done with you, whatever trick he's pulling, is working. You seem fine and healthy now, but should I be worried? Am I helping him by making you think this is okay?"

"I think he's changing. There's something different with him each time I see him. Each time I let him in, it's like he's becoming more human."

Or you are becoming more demon.

His comment rang deep within her, and her eyes traveled back to her room. To the nightstand, where the potion she'd received from Cían rested inside the drawer. Asmodeus was lying. He had to be. She'd felt his compassion when they saved Isaac. It wasn't her who was changing. He was.

Sarah hugged Leah, squeezing tight. "If you think you have this under control, then I'll stand by you. But don't think for a second that I won't drag that demon out of you myself if I think he's hurting you."

Tears welled up in Leah's eyes, and she squeezed Sarah. She was safe in Sarah's arms, the safest she'd felt since her parents died. Her best friend trusted Leah more than anyone ever had before.

Sarah let her go and wiped away her tears. "You're gonna have to fess up to Eric. If you think he's going to drop you off at some Infinity Board torture chamber, then I don't think you realize how much he cares about you. Tell him about Isaac, and how you're still in control. If you don't, and Gabe does, then there's no telling who will hear it and who will react. But if things go sour, then you, Isaac, and I will run off, and I'll clobber anyone who gets in our way."

"I won't let you two throw this all away because of me."

"Oh, I'm sorry. You think you have a choice?" Sarah cracked her knuckles.

"This was my secret," Leah said. "My problem. I chose to work with Asmodeus, knowing there would be consequences."

Sarah crossed her arms. "And those consequences will include myself and Isaac running off with you. So, deal with it."

Leah laughed. "Do you really think Isaac would agree with your plan?"

Sarah peered out the window. "Why don't we find out? Seems like the guards aren't out patrolling yet to yell at us about curfew. Let's check on him."

They stepped back inside the academy and tiptoed down the dark hall, slipping into the infirmary. The light beside Isaac's bed was turned on, and he held a book as they entered.

Leah couldn't help but stare at the thin black scar that traveled up his cheek, across his eye, and up past his hairline, leaving behind a streak of white hair. He was still paler than usual, and the lamplight didn't help him look any less gaunt, but he smiled as he saw them enter.

"Look who's awake," Sarah said as they rushed to his side.

"Oh, I'm so glad to see you," Isaac said, wrapping his arms around them. "What happened?"

Sarah glanced at Leah, then said, "It's a long story. What's the last thing you remember?"

Isaac paused, trying to collect his thoughts while

placing a finger on his lips. "There was a . . . kid. A boy. How is he? Is he all right?"

Leah nodded down to the darkened end of the infirmary. "He's hooked up down there. Still asleep, but stable. You saved him and almost got killed doing it."

Isaac pulled up his shirt, revealing the blackened scar on his stomach. "And this?"

"You got your ass possessed," Sarah said. "Well, kinda. Leah saved you and botched the ritual, which also almost killed you. They took the kid back here, and we went on a field trip." Sarah turned and paused, pushing up off Isaac's bed and taking a few steps toward the corner. "Wait. Where is he?"

Leah looked down at the last bed, squinting, and noticed it was empty. She turned to Isaac. "Has anyone else come in here?"

Isaac shook his head. "I just woke up. Sid must have left me a book in case I got up, but I haven't seen anyone."

Sarah went to the kid's bed and inspected it. "Bed's still warm. He didn't leave too long ago. Do you think maybe Constance had him moved?"

Something is wrong. Someone is coming. Asmodeus's voice echoed in Leah's head.

Leah's gut twisted, and time slowed. Imaginary ropes tied around her body as her control vanished and Asmodeus took over.

"Get down!" her voice tore through her, yelling at Sarah. She couldn't even think as she involuntarily leaped forward with inhuman speed. Leah's arms wrapped around Sarah, tackling her to the ground while protecting her head.

The glass from the window above them shattered, and a demon with long sharpened claws swatted at the empty air where Sarah had been. It landed with a thud on the infirmary floor and clamored to all fours like some feral animal.

The demon was a young woman with pale skin and red hair, but the bones of her spine tore through her flesh and clothes. She twisted her head backward toward them, revealing elongated teeth and torn lips.

Sharpened bone protruded from her bloodied fingertips. The demon hissed.

Then she lunged again.

CHAPTER 30

THE ASSAULT

Leah activated *Netzach*, and the claws glided across her face and arms like she was made of diamond.

Sarah's fist connected with the demon, a surge of energy tearing a hole through it.

The demon fell limp, knocking them to the floor, covering the two of them in blood. Sarah's eyes widened, and she stared at her blood covered fist. "I . . . I . . ."

Before either of them could react, another demon jumped through the window, landing on the empty bed. It let out a low growl before leaping at Isaac.

Leah hefted the dead body off her, but she knew she would be too late. She couldn't reach the demon before it got to Isaac.

The demon froze in midair. Leah shifted her gaze to Isaac, and he slowly got to his feet, his hands clapped together. He stood up and groaned. "Well, don't you look ugly?" Isaac then thrust out his hands, sending the demon catapulting back out the window.

With another *Malchut* push, he sent the row of beds tumbling toward the window, piling up and bending in on each other, effectively barricading them against whatever else wanted to come through.

Isaac leaned against his bed and held his hand at his naval, wincing.

"Isaac! Are you alright?" Sarah shouted as both she and Leah got to her feet.

"Yeah, I just got up too fast, I think. I'll be fine."

Scratching sounded from the other side of the pile of beds. Leah clenched her fists. "We have to go. Now! The others need to know we're—"

Nykima's voice blasted over the sound system. "Attention, we are under attack. This is not a drill. Assemble at the main entrance, now!"

Sid burst through the infirmary door, looking from Isaac to the window to Leah and Sarah wiping blood off their faces. "What are you two . . . never mind, it doesn't matter. Help me get Isaac out of here. Where's the kid?"

Leah shook her head. "He's not here. He wasn't here when we snuck in."

Sid let out a sigh while he approached Isaac, helping him put on his shoes before wrapping an arm around him and heading for the exit.

As they left the Infirmary, Leah heard metal sliding into place. The emergency barricades had been activated, and every window and door to the outside now had a layer of steel sliding into place, blocking off any intruder.

Bangs echoed through the halls from every direction as the four of them found Miranda and Joanna rushing down the stairs. Blood covered Joanna's clothes, and she spun her head around as thumping echoed off the walls. "What the fuck is going on?"

"Demons," Sid said. "I don't know how many, but by the sound of it, way more than we can handle."

Another loud bang at the front entrance, and the

wooden doors cracked. "Are we even safe here?" Miranda asked.

"Yeah," Joanna said. "Wouldn't the cells be safer? That has to be like a bunker, right?"

Leah looked to the cafeteria, where the entrance to the cells were and where Rigel probably sat, alone, with no idea of what was happening. "We should go help Rigel."

Sid shook his head. "Orders were to meet here. We can decide what to do after that."

Gabe, Brandon, and Ricardo arrived, all dressed in pajamas and combat boots.

Seconds after them, the doors of the offices creaked open, and Helen appeared at the steps, leading the others behind her.

"Pawns, prepare for battle," Helen said.

A scream sounded from the hallway leading to the infirmary, followed by footsteps as a bloodied demon raced into sight. Helen shot it a glance, and it instantly sliced in two, falling over dead.

Leah looked up at Helen in awe. The woman had barely moved to unleash *Malchut*. Leah had never seen that and thought it was damn near impossible, but Helen had done it without a second thought.

Helen continued. "It's likely that some demons have passed through the barricades, either before they were deployed or through sheer force. There's no time to even think about exorcism. We shoot to kill, and we travel in teams. Head to the armory and get what you need. There's no time to fully suit up, so don't bother."

"But what happened?" Isaac blurted out. His eyes widened as he looked at Helen. Even he was surprised by his own outburst, and he quickly lowered his head. "I'm sorry, Black Queen Nielsen."

She didn't directly acknowledge him, instead speaking

to everyone, "Demons have attacked the academy. Our guards are not responding, and it looks like they cut communications too. Even cell reception seems jammed. We don't know what the numbers are beyond that wall. Whoever planned this knew exactly how to keep us in the dark. I've sent out a couple of my personal guards to get reinforcements. In the meantime, we must stand our ground and protect each other. Understood?"

Everyone snapped their feet together and stood tall. "Yes, my Queen!"

Leah glanced back at the cafeteria. She wanted to ask again about Rigel, but the others had already started their way down the hall. She turned and walked right into Joanna.

"Woah, everything okay?" Joanna asked.

"Yeah, it's fine," Leah said. "Did you or the guards see anything when you were out there?"

Joanna shook her head. "I came back to warn the Queen. I don't think the guards stood a chance."

They caught up with the others, strapping on vests and belts over sweatpants and pajamas. Leah grabbed knives off the wall, sliding them into place on her belt, followed by an automatic rifle that she strapped over her shoulder and magazines on her vest.

Eric stepped up beside her, tightening her shoulder strap. "You can't save them. Understand?"

Leah turned her gun over and nodded. "I do. If it's between us and them, I choose us."

"Stay close to me."

She nodded, and Eric pulled a gun off the wall for himself.

Once everyone had what they needed, they joined back up at the entrance hall. None of them were suited up to the standards they had for missions. Almost all of them were wearing some type of sweatpants, jeans, or pajamas underneath vests, belts, and combat boots. But it would have to do.

Helen stepped out in front of them, now sporting a blue trench coat and no visible weapons. Leah wondered if she had any concealed under her coat, or if she'd rely only on the Tree of Life as a means of offense.

"We need to assess the perimeter," Helen said. "Nykima, Grace, you two will split—"

A boom tore through the entrance hall, and the wooden doors cracked and fell off their hinges, leaving behind the severely dented metal barricade.

Helen reached both hands into her trench coat and drew two katanas, holding them out on either side. "Brace yourselves!"

A second blow cracked the stone wall surrounding the door and the metal sheet. Leah readied her rifle. Her left arm twitched, and she felt an odd warmth billowing out from it.

Strange, Asmodeus said.

"What?"

These demons are using your Tree of Life. There are Mystics among them.

Leah's heart nearly jumped from her chest. *They have Mystics?!* One demon possessing a Mystic is dangerous enough, but facing off with multiple? Were they even prepared for that? She couldn't hold that in, couldn't risk not saying anything. "They've possessed Mystics!" Leah shouted.

Eric looked at her, eyebrows furrowed. "What? How do you—"

The metal barricade snapped off its hinges and crashed into the ground, billowing up into a cloud of dust.

"They're coming!" Helen warned.

CHAPTER 31

BREACH

Demons rushed in, climbing on the walls and ceiling. Some of their bodies appeared so contorted that they no longer looked human. Instead, they looked like massive fleshy spiders.

Helen pointed a katana at them. "Attack!"

Bullets fired at the entrance, connecting with demons and pulling them down from the walls and ceiling. Yet, for every demon that fell, it seemed another two appeared as more flooded the entrance.

Leah spotted the familiar clothes of a guard—a Mystic who was stationed to protect them.

She fired her gun, but the bullets simply bounced off him as he walked through the carnage of bodies.

Asmodeus spoke in her ear. *He's using Netzach and trying to divert your attention from the others.*

A loud explosion sounded from behind. Leah turned and saw the barricade that covered the doors to the field shook and cracked against the foundation. Another crash sounded above, and Sid, Isaac, and Brandon rushed up the stairs, seeking cover as an onslaught of demons that crawled in from the second story.

Leah, behind you!

She spun around, spotting a demon racing toward her with inhuman speed. It was too fast. She wouldn't be able to bring up her gun in time. She wouldn't be able to—

The blade of a katana sliced cleanly through the demon as Helen materialized in front of Leah.

"Focus on the front and trust the others to have your six!" Helen shouted. Then, she vanished again in a whoosh of air, only to reappear near the entrance, cutting down another demon before vanishing again. She appeared halfway up the wall to engulf another creature in flames.

Chokmah. Teleportation. So, this was the power of a Queen. Leah had to stop focusing on her, but her chest expanded, a warm feeling inside. There was still hope. They could win this fight.

The demons pressed closer, and Leah lowered her gun, instead focusing on the energy rising inside herself. *Malchut* formed at the end of her fingertips, and she cut through the air, pulsing short blades that cut into the mass of demons scrambling toward her. She tore off the arm of a large man, one of the guards, and before she could stop to think about who he was, three more demons climbed over him.

Another loud bang brought with it a rumble beneath her feet, and Leah knew the back doors had crumbled. She looked over her shoulder to see Constance, Grace, and Sarah rushing toward the rear entrance. Fire covered Sarah's arms, and as the first demons came in, a torrent of flames met them.

She turned back to the front, ready to fend off any demons that crept closer. What she didn't expect was a massive, fleshy spider dropping from the ceiling.

It pinned Leah to the ground, its boney legs protruding from bloody flesh and broken ribs moving as if it were a second mouth. The demon screamed at her, thick bloody drool streaming from its maw. It pressed down on Leah, holding her hands in place and lifting a long leg, ready to strike her dead.

A gunshot sounded from her left, and the demon seized up and fell to the side. She wriggled free and saw Eric, covered in cuts of his own, his eyes wide.

Before he could utter a word, another demon fell from the ceiling and lunged at Eric.

Asmodeus moved faster than Eric or Leah, extending Leah's hand, using *Nehemoth* to pull the demon off its course and toward Leah. Energy flooded her right arm, and she sent a right hook filled with *Malchut* into the demon's face, knocking its head off entirely.

Eric stared, stunned for a moment, before approaching and pulling her up. "We've got to fall back."

Asmodeus held control of Leah's arm, pulling demons off walls. Leah controlled her other arm, using *Malchut* with her uncle to cut down demons as they raced toward the stairs. What should have only been a few feet felt like traveling for an eternity as demons kept blocking their path and surrounding them.

They pushed through the last wave before the steps, and Leah spotted Ricardo.

He lay on his backside on the stairs, eyes wide open, lifeless. Blood poured from the gash in his throat and a demon sat atop him, tearing at his insides.

Leah slashed her hand, sending a *Malchut* slice that cut the demon's body in half.

She stared into Ricardo's dead eyes and stumbled back off down the stairs.

Eric grabbed her arm. "We have to keep moving."

"But . . . Ricardo. He's—"

"Leah, now!" Eric launched another *Malchut* push, knocking back the wall of demons clamoring to reach them.

One demon, a short woman wearing a hijab, didn't falter from the hit. By the looks of her clothes, she was a Mystic. She growled, baring bloodied teeth as she lifted a fist and aimed it right at Leah.

Asmodeus wrapped his hand around the woman's fist, and Leah felt the *Malchut* energy release from the demon.

It should have ripped off Leah's arm and torn her to bits. Instead, Asmodeus called on *Nehemoth,* and that energy pulled right into her, filling her for a second before she sent it right back.

The woman's arm cracked in several places, bones protruding out of her skin, before the demon lifted off the ground. The push sent Leah flying back and crashing through the cafeteria doors as the demon flung backward into the hall.

Leah felt a moment of weightlessness before landing, hard, on her back. She blinked a few times, gasping for air and tasting blood in her mouth. Running her fingers up her side, Leah winced as she felt her ribs. She must have cracked them. The pain was intense, and every time Leah breathed, it felt like a knife stabbing her in the chest.

Get up! Asmodeus shouted.

Leah felt searing hot pain as she pushed herself up on her elbows. The agony traveled down her back and to her hips.

She looked around, noting that the cafeteria was completely empty, free from the pandemonium just beyond the doors.

As she turned to the doorway, she saw the woman with her hijab covered in blood, pushing through the demons that clamored toward Eric. The demon's eyes trained on Leah, her right arm dangling at her side, clearly broken beyond repair.

Eric raced over as the woman lumbered into the cafeteria. He raised his gun and shot her, but the bullet bounced off. The demon turned and waved its unharmed hand, and Eric was flung back into the mayhem. She turned toward Leah.

Leah tried to catch her breath while pulling herself up, but the pain was too great. Her attacker rushed in, a large sneer across her face as she lifted her hand once more. Leah saw the way the woman held her hand and knew she was readying to cut her down with *Malchut*.

If you want to make it out of here, give me control. Now!

Leah shut her eyes, her heart beating in her chest. "Do it!"

Her body jerked against her will as Asmodeus took over. The pain made her want to scream, but no matter how much she tried, her body didn't respond to her. It wasn't hers anymore.

Leah stood, feeling every crunch of her bones as they stacked on top of each other, clearly broken. Her lungs filled with air, pushing against cracked ribs and breathing past the point of pain she'd ever imagined.

The demon swung its hand down, energy tearing through her fingers.

At the same moment, Leah's hands clasped together. Not dissimilar to *Hod*, but instead of her hands clapping together and her fingers pointing up, knuckles pressed into her open palm and one set of fingers aimed toward Leah's chest while the other aimed directly at the demon.

Leah faced the demon, her body tense with anticipation as the demon's *Malchut* attack flew toward her. The demon's face twisted into a sneer as the attack hit Leah square in the chest, and both of them were momentarily frozen in place. She braced herself for the slashing pain, but nothing came. The woman focused on her, and Leah felt the rage emanating off her. Anger filled Leah. A hatred for the thing standing in front of her. Why did it deserve to live while she was about to die? Her chest breathed in and out, pressing harder and harder against her broken ribs.

The more she breathed, the less pain emanated from her ribs. That feeling flowed down her spine and to her hips, a warmth that seemed to ease the ache with every breath. She was healing, her bones stitching back together with each slow, deep breath.

She could hear the chaos outside the cafeteria door, flying bodies and the flash of gunfire, completely unaware of what happened here between Leah and this demon.

Leah focused on the demon, still trapped in her hold. The creature's eyes bulged, and veins protruded from her neck.

She let out a raspy breath, and blood trickled out of the woman's mouth.

Leah breathed in life again while the demon sputtered out blood. The more air Leah breathed, the more the demon in front crumbled. Blood poured from her eyes as her knees trembled.

That's enough, Leah told Asmodeus.

"Just a little more," Asmodeus whispered through Leah's lips. He held the position, drawing in more breaths. Any fatigue Leah had vanished, and she felt better than she had in months.

Asmodeus dropped his hands, and with it, his hold on the demon gave way. The possessed Mystic fell forward, face slamming into the ground, dead.

Ropes reformed in Leah's mind, and her body became her own once again. She opened and closed her fists, feeling this newfound energy surging through her.

"What the hell was that?"

Samael, opposite to Hod. Instead of changing energy, you absorb it. In this case, her life.

Leah felt at her ribs, which no longer ached, and she took in a breath that she fully controlled. She stared at the dead woman, guilt creeping into her mind.

We have to go, Asmodeus said.

Leah nodded and started toward the door.

Her footsteps froze of their own accord, and Asmodeus said, *Wait. I think I see it now.*

"See what? We have to get back and help the others."

Legion wouldn't attack like this. He works in the shadows, slowly turning everyone he can until the world is his. He's more cunning. Possessing guards that were clearly aware of the Queen's presence and still launching a full-on assault? He's wasting too much to just get inside. Why?

Leah looked at the dead body, then back toward the broken doors that led out to the entrance. "And why hasn't anything broken in through the cafeteria? Demons are spilling in from everywhere but here. If they came through those doors, that would have really screwed up our position."

Perhaps it is all a diversion?

That word made something click in Leah's head. She spun around and raced into the kitchen. As she'd expected, the door to the cellar was propped wide open.

"They wanted Rigel," she whispered as she rushed down the steps.

She fumbled for the switch on her way down, the bulb flickering to life as she reached the bottom steps.

A high-pitched voice sounded from the shadows. "It took you long enough."

The room brightened around Leah. She spotted the child they'd saved standing in the shadows, holding a knife and surrounded by an aura of black obsidian that shone light back at her. "What are you?"

"Death." The child brought down his knife over and

over onto the mass in front of him. It screamed, and Leah watched as Rigel thrashed and bleated as he tried to break free from the child.

"Bastard!" Leah launched herself forward with *Malchut*, readying her arm to push him through the wall.

The energy in her hand immediately sapped from her, and bloody marks glowed on the ground, tracing up the walls and onto the ceiling as she landed within a ritual circle. She froze in her tracks, aware of the mistake she'd made.

The child smirked. "Oh, don't worry. This is an evocation, not a possession. I simply needed one of you to activate it."

Rigel screamed as light shone through his chest. His body lifted off the floor, and the light within him grew brighter and brighter. Shrieking sounds cut through the air, and Leah covered her ears, trying to block the screams to no avail.

Energy flowed past Leah, first like a small trickle and then a raging river. It pulled on her, dragging her closer to Rigel. She fell to her knees, keeping herself in place as the energy surged.

It stopped as quickly as it had begun. She looked up to see Rigel's hovering body, the light now a thin line tracing from the tip of his head down to the space between his feet.

Run! Now! Asmodeus said.

Sparks of light crackled out from the line, striking the concrete floor and splitting the walls.

Rigel looked at Leah, his mouth muttering unspoken words. Then a shadowed hand materialized from the line, protruding from Rigel's chest. The chimera let out a guttural scream, his eyes wide as another hand materialized from within the line. The hands grasped onto either side of the stretched line, and pulled, tearing Rigel apart and leaving a hole of light hovering in the air.

A shadowed leg stepped through, and Asmodeus screamed in Leah's head, *Run, Leah! Now!*

She pushed up to her feet, readying to turn when the shadowed hand lifted. She froze in place, against her will, her muscles locked.

The thing stepped completely out from the hole in the shape of a man, but as if whatever was supposed to be there had been cut from reality, leaving behind a black hole instead.

The child bowed. "Master. You have arrived. We are all prepared for what comes next."

"Excellent. Many thanks to you, Miss Ackerman, for opening the door." His voice was hoarse and low.

Leah immediately recognized it. Flashes of her standing in a room with long drawn curtains and a fireplace, and then again in a room underground, full of candles with a screaming old man tied in the center.

"Legion," Leah whispered. The shadow tilted his head, and though Leah couldn't see it, she knew his smile had to be wide as he looked at her.

A silvery chain materialized in Legion's hand. "In the flesh."

CHAPTER 32
LEGION

The chain flew through the air, aimed right at Leah's head. She couldn't move, couldn't dodge out of the way. She was frozen in place by Legion's hold on her. Even Asmodeus couldn't save her now. She was going to die, and there was nothing she or anyone else could do to stop it.

A hand wrapped around Leah's chest and squeezed tight. One second, the chain was mere inches from her head. The next, all reality tore apart. She was nowhere and everywhere all at once. She felt hot sand on her face and freezing cold snow at her feet. Heard the cheers of some sporting event and the cries as a pastor gave last rites. She heard everything, felt everything. The universe was hers.

Then, as quickly as it had happened, it all vanished and she crumpled to the floor of the main entrance to the academy.

She caught her bearings at the foot of the main stairs, noting the other Mystics surrounding her and that Helen had her arm wrapped around her. Leah whipped her head left and right, expecting the onslaught of demons to leap at her any second, but the hall was devoid of demon life. Only bodies lay, contorted and dead, on the entrance's marble floor. Her gaze went to the broken door, and the eyes of demons, standing shoulder to shoulder, stared at her . . . waiting.

"Leah!" Sarah and Isaac raced down the steps and helped Leah to her feet.

Helen stood firm and looked at the cafeteria entrance. "Brace yourselves."

A piercing scream sounded from the kitchen, and the floors trembled.

Eric stepped in front of Leah and her friends. Blood covered his face, but his amber eyes stayed set ahead.

"Legion is here," Helen said.

A giant chain crashed through the stone floor, sending debris everywhere. A second and third crash tore through the cafeteria's walls, turning it into a heap of rubble.

We aren't ready for this. We need to run! Asmodeus screamed.

Leah gripped her pistol, looking around at her team. They'd already lost Ricardo, and by the looks of it, Joanna was gone too. They were all covered in blood, beaten, and bruised, but no one else backed down.

Her gaze met Gabe's but quickly swept past him toward the cafeteria. Legion had come in here, attacked them, and destroyed the place she'd called home for nearly a year. She shook her head and whispered to Asmodeus. "No. We aren't running. We're going to fight."

The cloud of dust settled, and Legion stepped out of the rubble that was once the cafeteria. The chains once holding him back were gone.

Helen leaped forward, vanishing and reappearing a foot away from Legion. She swung both her katanas at his neck.

He dodged them with inhuman speed, twisting his

body and slamming a fist into Helen's side. The Queen flew backward, crashing into the wall.

"Queen's Gambit, protect your Queen!" Constance demanded. "Kill Legion!" She rushed forward, slamming her hands into the ground and screaming as tree roots burst from the earth beneath Legion, twisting and wrapping around him.

Sarah, Nykima, Grace, Miranda, and Brandon leaped down the stairs toward Legion, sending waves of fire while Sid and Isaac clapped their hands, their eyes trained on Legion. Gabe followed beside them, his gaze switching between the waiting demons and Legion, ready to protect Sid and Isaac no matter what.

Leah ran beside Eric, dropping her pistol and filling herself with anger and pressure. They sent *Malchut* cuts, one after the other, then dodged out of the way for Brandon, Miranda, and Gabe to hit the demon with a second wave.

They attacked in unison, the many evenings of practice paying off, sending energy that crashed down on Legion. The burning tree roots continued climbing up his neck and tightening, creating a coffin of fire.

Legion didn't move as the roots closed over his head.

Leah looked at Constance, who kept her eyes trained on the burning roots.

Then a raspy laugh echoed through the room, followed by his hoarse voice. "Is that all you've got?"

In one move, Legion broke free from the *Hod* Isaac and Sid had on him, sending them stumbling back while the demon snapped himself free of the roots. The bright orange fires burning the roots changed to black before he raised his arms and sent the flames billowing out in all directions.

Leah dodged the incoming flames, hiding behind an

overturned couch. The fire slammed into the couch, consuming it in seconds.

She looked back at the others and heard a scream. Brandon hadn't been as lucky. He rolled on the ground as the flames engulfed him like some wild animal.

She pushed off the ground, ready to do anything in her power to put him out, but Eric grabbed her arm. "No! Black flames will spread to you if you help him."

They were going to lose. Legion had the upper hand. Leah then had a thought.

"The potion!" Leah screamed. It was still upstairs, tucked away in her nightstand.

We don't have time—

Demons flooded in from the main entrance. Sid, Isaac, and Gabe turned to face them, working together as a fluid team, cutting down the oncoming monsters.

"We have to get it," Leah muttered, pushing up from the couch.

Constance stood, pulling her arms up into the air as new growth wrapped around Legion. She held her hands out toward Legion and crossed her arms. The roots attacked, trying to pierce and rip him apart as black flames engulfed them.

"Flank to Sid!" Eric shouted at Leah and launched off the ground.

Leah scaled across the lobby and landed next to him, joining in the battle against the torrent of demons flooding in.

She peered past the demons. "If I can get through here and—"

No, we can't leave our back exposed to him! Asmodeus shouted.

He pulled her arm back, aiming at the blackened flames that ate away at Brandon's corpse.

Her arm surged with energy, and the black flames leaped from Brandon's body into her hands. It was cold to her, almost like the flames feared burning her.

"Leah!" Eric shouted. "What are you doing?"

Her hand thrust forward, and the black fire shot into the crowd of demons, spreading to each one that stood in the doorway.

They screamed and burned. Then she felt the pull of *Nehemoth* as Asmodeus brought down the roof above the main doors.

Sid turned and looked at Leah, his eyes wide and mouth agape.

Eric looked Leah over. His eyes flashed yellow as they fell on her left arm. "All that and your arm is the only thing that looks corrupt. Wait . . . is it . . . vanishing?"

The chance for conversation ended when cracking wood sounded behind them.

They all turned and saw Legion, still entombed in a burning cocoon of roots, his face staring at Constance.

Then the mass of roots and fire surrounding him disintegrated, and Legion's silvery chains lay glistening on the floor.

He didn't move, but his chains launched forward, targeting Constance.

The White Bishop raised a hand and used *Malchut* to knock them off course, but they coiled around, like living snakes pursuing their prey.

Eric launched off the ground and stood near Constance, joining her in blocking the chains.

They knocked another set of chains off course, and Constance shouted, "Get Helen!"

Sid looked at Leah, then back at Helen, and pulled on Isaac's arm.

Gabe kept his eyes on Leah, his jaw working but no words coming out.

"Gabe, to me!" Sid shouted.

Sid led Isaac and Gabe along the wall, keeping as much distance as he could, while Constance and Eric sliced and blocked Legion's attempt to subdue her or shift his target to Isaac.

Leah spotted Nykima and Grace, with Sarah and Miranda, flanking Legion to the side and launching another torrent of orange flames.

Legion didn't budge. Instead, his chains vanished in an instant and his face turned toward them, waving a hand that sent a pulse of *Malchut* so strong it threw rubble and chunks of concrete at them.

Sarah and Grace dodged them, but Nykima and Miranda weren't as lucky. A large concrete slab slammed into them and sent them flying. Nykima landed on a heap of rubble, and Miranda slammed into the stone wall with a loud, audible crack. Her body crumpled to the ground, blood marking the wall where she landed.

Move! Asmodeus shouted as a second wave of *Malchut* flew at Leah, rubble pulled up in its force.

She focused on *Malchut,* pooling it into her feet, and jumped high in the air, over the wave of energy Legion had sent her way, using *Netzach* to land easily next to Nykima. Blood seeped through Nykima's clothes from her side. Leah tore off the bottom half of her shirt and wrapped it around Nykima's waist, tying it tight against the wound.

Nykima let out a gasp and met Leah's gaze, holding her arm. "My legs . . . I can't . . ." Her eyes rolled to the back of her skull, and she passed out.

The sound of chains rattling pulled Leah's attention back to Legion. In quick succession, he whipped Eric away, like swatting at a fly, and made contact with Constance, wrapping his chains tight against her torso. He pulled, and she stumbled forward.

Constance wriggled against the chains and let out a scream. Her hands burst into flames, and she clawed at the chains. The fire glowed a bright white, and the scent of burning flesh filled the air. But the chains remained intact, glowing red.

He pulled her again, bringing her closer to him.

Sid, Isaac, and Gabe helped Helen get away from Legion, dragging her back near the collapsed entrance. Sid held his hands over Helen while Isaac and Gabe joined him on either side.

"You're their leader, yes?" Legion asked. "You have been looking for me." He pulled Constance in closer. "Well, here I am."

CHAPTER 33

CHECKMATE

Leah pointed her hand forward and focused all her energy into one tiny point. Asmodeus sucked in energy, frost forming on the surrounding ground. Then she released, and it shot through the air, piercing through Legion's shoulder and forcing him to step back.

Leah cradled her hand, the pressure sending zaps of pain from her joints.

Legion focused on Leah, outstretching his other hand. Chains slithered out from the shadows. "I should have killed you when I had the chance!"

Grace took that opportunity to leap from Legion's side, her fist aimed at his head. It connected, and the energy that pushed out from her hand sent a shockwave that reverberated in Leah's chest.

Legion didn't move, and Grace fell to the ground beside him, holding her crumpled hand.

Legion cocked his head and held a hand out to Grace, the other still holding firm on Constance's chain leash. "What was it you tried to do to me? Ah, yes."

Chains slipped down his open hand and slithered around Grace, wrapping around her arms and legs and lifting her off the ground. Grace screamed as the chains enveloped her broken hand, and her other hand lit on fire, billowing flames into Legion's face.

The chains tightened around Grace, and she let out a gasp, the flames snuffing out. Her eyes locked on Legion's face, and even though the chains squeezed more, Grace didn't scream. She moved against them, pulling them away from her neck.

Grace lifted her hand, resisting the pull of the chains with the strength of *Netzach*.

She hit him again with *Malchut*. And again. Hit after hit, slamming into him and sending shock waves into the air.

Legion turned and looked at Constance, ignoring the hits from Grace. "Is this the best you can do?"

Grace gasped, her *Netzach* reaching its limit. The chains squeezed tight against soft flesh, crushing her into pieces in an instant.

"No!" Sarah shouted a few feet from Leah. She slumped to her knees, her hands shaking as she clutched at her heart, feeling the death of her Bishop pass through her bond.

Legion gave the chain one last pull, and Constance pressed up against Legion's shadowed body. She stared at the space Grace had been seconds before, tears streaming down her face. Legion lifted a finger to her chin and pulled her face to his. "I have something far more special in store for you."

He wrapped his arms around her. Constance let out a scream as his arms squeezed.

Leah watched in horror as Constance phased into Legion, as if he truly was a black void, and Constance was about to be consumed into nothingness.

Her screams echoed in the space, and Leah squeezed her eyes shut as Constance disappeared.

Leah, we have to get out of here, Asmodeus said. *We aren't strong enough. If you want to live, we have to run!*

Helen pushed off Sid, grabbing her swords again and lunging forward, vanishing, and reappearing at Legion's side. She cut into his shadowed side and punched him with *Malchut.* He stammered back before swatting a clawed hand at her, but she vanished again before he could connect.

Leah looked back at Sarah, still sitting on her knees, her eyes glossed over from losing her Bishop. Then Leah met Isaac's eyes from across the room and they nodded, both pushing off the ground and going to Sarah.

Their fear for their friend must have reverberated through their bonds, because the instant they went to her, Eric and Sid moved in tandem, sending *Malchut* waves toward Legion and keeping them covered. Gabe joined Sid's side, distracting Legion as much as they could.

"Come on," Isaac said. "We have to get you somewhere safe. Get up."

"She was . . . She can't . . . How?" Tears fell from Sarah's face as Leah and Isaac dragged her back to Nykima.

Isaac looked at Leah. "What do we do? He's going to kill all of us."

Leah shook her head and stared at Legion. A small head peeking out of the rubble caught her eye—the child demon, his eyes glowing red as he looked at Legion.

She squeezed her eyes tight. *Is it possible that the kid is helping Legion somehow?*

Asmodeus didn't answer. Instead, warmth billowed from behind her eyes, and she snapped them open, focusing on the child. A red line connected the boy to Legion.

She blinked and turned to Isaac. "There's another

demon. I think he's protecting Legion somehow. If I can get to him, we might be able to end this."

Isaac nodded. "I'll join in the distraction."

Cold gel washed over her, and the sounds of battle muted in her ears. A strange, yellowed full moon shone down through holes in the ceiling, instead of the half-moon she's seen before. Yellow moss cushioned her feet, and the stale air made her sick. She saw Isaac stand and leave her, clapping his hands together.

She turned and ran alongside the walls, racing past Legion and creeping along the back wall toward the rubble heap that was once the cafeteria.

There, she saw him—the little boy, his eyes locked on Legion with his fingers interlaced, muttering words under his breath.

She stepped closer, and a figure stepped out from the rocks. Joanna. Her eyes burned yellow as she stared down at Leah's feet. "Woah there, ghosty. Where do you think you're going?"

Leah dropped the invisibility and raised an eyebrow at her. "Joanna? I thought you were dead. What are you doing?"

Joanna's head cocked to the side, and she smiled wide. "Joanna's not here anymore. Hasn't been here for a while."

Silvery light caught her eye, and she looked at Legion, his face directed at her, a chain flying in her direction.

Asmodeus reached out Leah's left arm, and Leah felt the pull of *Nehemoth* as a giant heap of concrete came flying at her. It crashed into the chain, knocking it off course and onto the ground at her feet.

Helen appeared at Legion's side, slicing her blade through his leg. Small, thorny vines tore through the ground and wrapped around his legs. He fought against them, stumbling to his knees as she shouted, "Your fight is with me!"

Joanna landed a punch to Leah's ribs and sent her flying back. She landed on her back as fire flew over her head.

"You won't lay another fucking hand on her!" Isaac yelled, flinging a wall of fire at Joanna. Isaac raced up beside Leah and clapped his hands.

Leah pushed up to her feet and launched off the ground, punching Joanna in the face and sending her flying through the crumbled wall into the cafeteria.

The clang of chains and swords between Helen and Legion carried on. Energy built up in her body as she turned to find the kid, but he'd already vanished beneath the rubble.

Her eyes locked on Joanna. "I know you're still in there, Joanna. Fight against it. We can help you."

Joanna sat up and smiled. "Your friend is gone." She leaped up and sent a blast of *Malchut* toward the cafeteria ceiling, sending debris everywhere.

Leah backed up, her eyes on the rubble until she found her friends again. Helen appeared at Leah's side, clutching Gabe. "Hurry and gather everyone. We have to get out of here."

Gabe looked at Leah, confused by the sudden teleportation, and Helen vanished once again. Leah looked toward Legion and saw Eric and Sid still on the other side of the cafeteria, distracting Legion with flying heaps of concrete as Helen flitted around the foyer.

Gabe stood and raised his fist, ready to take on Legion again.

"Go!" Sid shouted from across the room, his eyes locked on Gabe. "That's an order!"

Legion laughed, knocking the stones away like they

were nothing. Helen swooped in for another cut at Legion before more debris flew his way.

As they joined back up with Nykima, who still lay on the debris, Leah noted that Eric and Sid's *Malchut* attacks slowed. She suspected their energy was dwindling and worried what would happen if they ran out.

Leah got up and ran toward Eric.

"What are you doing?" he shouted.

"I'm not leaving you!" She readied herself, filling *Malchut* into her fists.

Anger rumbled through their bond, and he aimed a hand in her direction, hitting her with a wave of *Malchut* that sent her sliding backward. "Get back with the others!"

"Now!" Helen yelled as she sliced her blades past Legion's torso.

Eric and Sid propelled themselves across the lobby and landed between the others and Legion. They clapped their hands together and broadened their stance. Veins protruded from their arms, and Legion's actions decelerated.

Chains soared through the air, moving slower and slower as they reached their targets. But they didn't stop in time. Leah watched as the chains pierced through both Eric and Sid before coming to a complete halt.

Sid fell to one knee, blood pouring from his mouth. He held his hands tight together.

The chains inched forward, tearing a hole through Eric's shoulder.

Pain ratcheted through Leah, an agony she hadn't felt before.

"Go!" Eric screamed. "Get out of here!"

Leah stepped toward her uncle, but Isaac grabbed her hand and pulled her back as tears streamed down his face. "We—We can't save them."

Eric held his stance firm as Sid fell forward. Eric screamed as the chains dug into his gut before halting again.

Eric turned, looking back at Leah. His eyes filled with tears. "I'm sorry."

Helen wrapped her arm around Leah, but she fought against it, staring at Eric.

"No, please," she muttered.

Eric gave her a half smile, and the hold he had on the chains gave way. They tore through him in seconds.

"No!" Leah screamed, as the reality around her shattered.

CHAPTER 34
A REAL SACRIFICE

Leah gasped as the world around her stitched itself back together, and she landed on a soft patch of grass. Pain roared through her chest, ripping her heart in two. She couldn't breathe, and everything spun around her. She gulped in cold air and felt her knees slamming into soft dirt.

Helen fell along with her, panting and struggling to stand. "We're at the edge of the woods. I couldn't bring us to the docks. Too far. We have to go. Now!"

Leah kept her hand to her chest and looked back at the academy, dimly lit by the half moon, seeing it crumbled and surrounded by dozens of demons clamoring to get in. The pain shot through her rib cage with every breath, and the image of Eric's face replayed in her head again. She had to get back and heal him. He wasn't gone. He couldn't be.

She stumbled to her feet, feeling as if she were moving through water, and turned toward the academy, her hands curled into fists.

A hand grabbed her wrist. "Leah, he's gone," Helen said.

Leah pulled away from Helen's grasp. "No! He could still be in there. We have to go back. We have to—"

"Listen to me," the Queen said, pulling herself up and grabbing Leah's shoulders. "Legion is too strong. There is nothing we can do. Eric died to protect us. To protect you."

Tears flowed down Leah's face, and she tried to pull away from Helen, but the Queen pulled her in close, wrapping her arms around her. "Let me go! Why didn't you save them!? Why didn't you stay and fight?"

Helen's grip tightened. "If we stayed, we'd all be dead. Eric sacrificed himself to save us. They all did. Do you want to stay here and let their sacrifice be for nothing? Or fall back, live, and get our revenge when we're ready?"

Leah heard sobs coming from behind her. When she looked, she saw Sarah, Isaac, and Gabe, all with the same pained look she knew she had on her face.

Leah slumped in Helen's arms, her voice cracking. "He was all I had left of her. All I had left of my mom."

Sarah pushed herself up, her face bloodied, and her eyes filled with tears. She grabbed Gabe's arm and pulled him up. "Help me carry Nykima. We need to go. We can't stay here."

Helen nodded, steering Leah to her side and taking up Isaac's silent offer to help her as they stepped into the woods.

Hours, minutes, or seconds could have passed by, but it didn't really matter to Leah. They walked through the woods, down familiar trails covered in grime and blood.

Asmodeus finally spoke with a silent whisper. *We weren't ready. I'm sorry.*

The dock came into view, a silhouette against the river behind it. Isaac pointed to the boathouse. "There should still be a johnboat and oars in there that aren't destroyed. Let's get it in the water."

Gabe and Isaac pulled out a flat-bottomed aluminum boat and dragged it to the water's edge.

Isaac and Gabe helped Sarah carry Nykima inside. Leah guided Helen, finding seats on the metal benches before Isaac pushed them away from the shore.

They sat in silence as Gabe rowed, sticking to the center of the river and following the bends as they flowed away from the academy.

Leah saw the orange light of flames off in the distance as the academy burned. Her home for the past year, gone.

Once they broke free from the woods, and they could see the glow of city lights ahead on the river, Helen pulled out a phone from her pocket and held it up. "Finally, some reception." She dialed a number and waited for a moment. "Black Queen Nielsen speaking, we're in a dead position. Do you hear me? Dead position and in critical condition. We need an extraction team, now."

The Queen waited for a response, her body tense. A muffled voice sounded over the phone, and she relaxed. "Colby, you're there. We're out of the academy. On the river. Can you and the other Knights converge on my point?" She shut her eyes for a second and drew in a breath. "I know. I felt it." A few seconds later, she responded. "Okay, we'll meet there." Then she hung up and pointed down the river, wincing and clutching her side with her other hand. "Down the river, six miles ahead, right before the nearest town."

"Queen Helen, are you okay?" Leah asked, turning in her seat.

Helen's face grew pale before she coughed up blood and slumped over in her seat.

"No!" Leah yelled.

Isaac caught her before she tumbled into the water, and they rocked back and forth, nearly flipping the whole boat. "Queen Helen! Can you hear me?"

Leah grabbed on to Helen, helping Isaac reposition her.

Warm, dark liquid pooled over her hands. She turned and looked at Gabe. "How long until we get there?"

"I don't know!" Gabe said as he picked up his pace, rowing.

Leah wasn't about to lose someone else. Not tonight. She looked at her friends. "We don't have enough time. We have to use *Chesed*. Now!"

Isaac and Leah laid Helen down, and Leah cradled Helen's head in her lap in the back of the boat. Sarah positioned herself near Helen's feet while Isaac stayed at her side.

Leah shut her eyes, pulling up memories between her and Helen. Helen had been there when Alma died. She took time to ensure Leah would be okay. She cared. Helen knew what Leah felt and had done everything she could to make Leah feel like she was a part of something bigger. If anyone deserved to be a Queen, Leah knew it was Helen.

Leah imagined the bright glow of energy surfacing inside her, but she felt nothing.

Helen's body lay still beneath them, and Leah couldn't muster the compassion it took to heal her. She'd failed her. Failed her Queen. Failed Eric. She couldn't let her die.

She wouldn't.

Leah replayed the memories in her head, trying with all her might to pull even a drop of energy from the Tree.

"Fuck!" Sarah screamed, slamming a fist to the side of the boat.

Isaac grabbed Leah's hand. "Our bonds. It's not working because we don't have our bonds."

"No," Leah said, shutting her eyes and focusing on her memories. "No one else is dying tonight! I can't. I won't. Please, stay with us."

Leah focused inward, searching for even a sliver of hope. She remembered how it should feel, the warmth bubbling up inside her, the pressure and electricity on her skin.

Leah, stop or we'll both die!

She shook her head. "Please, Helen. Stay with me. Please," Leah repeated, tugging at the hole in her chest.

She opened her eyes, hoping to see hands glowing a golden hue. Instead, the silvery moonlight shone, highlighting the blood stains. Her head spun, her eyes growing heavy as she still pushed herself to call on *Chesed*.

"I think I see them!" Gabe's voice sounded far away.

"I . . . have to . . . save her," Leah said, a flicker of golden light shining somewhere deep inside her.

"Please," she whispered as her eyes closed and she sank into darkness.

A Small Request From Us, The Authors

Thank you for continuing Leah's journey. We hope you've enjoyed it, so far.

As independent authors, reviews are so important to spread the word and reach new readers.

If you have a few seconds to spare, would you please consider leaving an honest review on the website you bought this book?

Your support helps so much in continuing Leah's story and the many others we plan to write in this world.

All the best,

A.B. Cohen & JP Rindfleisch IX

THE ASTRAL LAYERS
SHORT STORY

Go beyond Leah Ackerman

Delve into a secret world, an impending alliance, and a common enemy. From the shared universe of the Leah Ackerman series, check out this short story now!

https://BookHip.com/QQTLNDW

DORMANT ROOK

LEAH ACKERMAN SERIES BOOK FOUR

The story continues:

https://abcohenwrites.com/dormant-rook

CURSED JADE
AN ERIC MIZRAHI NOVELETTE

Get it free using the link below:

https://abcohenwrites.com/cursed-jade

ACKNOWLEDGMENTS

We would like to give our deepest thanks to everyone who has continued to support and help us throughout the creation of this third installment in the Leah Ackerman series. Your support, feedback, and encouragement have been invaluable.

A special shout out to our wonderful and steadfast team of editors, proofreaders, and designers, including J. Thorn, Zach Bohannon, Lori Diederich, and Getcovers.com. Your ongoing assistance and dedication to Leah Ackerman's story have been crucial in bringing this series to life.

A.B. Cohen here; as you may have noticed, our book is dedicated to someone truly special - Boris Sacks Z"L, the father of two of our Beta readers (and my cousins). Boris always carried a smile on his face, and his kindness was infectious. He had a passion for reading stories like the one you're holding in your hands and he passed on this love of literature to his amazing daughters. It is thanks to their dedication and support that you are able to enjoy the best version of our story. Sadly, Boris left us too soon and unexpectedly. However, his spirit will always be with us, and what better way to honor him than to spread the same kindness he exuded on a daily basis. I invite you, dear reader, to join us in carrying on Boris's legacy by performing a small act of kindness in his memory. Together, we can keep his spirit alive forever. Te quiero tío.

JP here; I'd like to express my gratitude for the thriving local author community that has blossomed around Maze

Books. Dave, you especially have been a cornerstone to the awesome growth in the writing community in Rockford. Your camaraderie and collaborative spirit have been a source of inspiration and motivation.

Lastly, we want to thank you, our incredible readers, for joining us on Leah's adventures. We hope you've enjoyed Deceived Bishop as much as we've enjoyed writing it, and we can't wait for you to see what comes next, in Dormant Rook, book four of the Leah Ackerman series!

Thank you all.

A.B. Cohen & JP Rindfleisch IX

About the Authors

A.B. Cohen is an author of freaky stories for weird people. He focus mainly on thrillers, horror and urban fantasy tales. Originally from Caracas, Venezuela, today he lives in Berkeley, California. Along with his passion for writing, he also loves dancing, soccer, and traveling. You can find out more about A.B. Cohen's upcoming writing projects using the link below:

www.abcohenwrites.com

JP Rindfleisch IX is a horror, urban fantasy, and science fiction writer. They live in Rockford, Illinois, with their partner of eleven years, and a menagerie of animal children including a Siberian husky, miniature dachshund, African grey parrot, Quaker parrot, and a run of the mill cat. They love creating art, nerding out over science, video games, tabletop RPGs, and spending hours in the kitchen crafting delectable vegan grub. You can learn more about JP Rindfleisch IX by following the link below:

www.jprindfleischix.com